*"So the w[...]
your hare[...]*

Jessica glanced at Kardahl, daring a contradiction.

He had sought comfort in the arms of many and achieved it with none. Kardahl thought there was no point in correcting her misconception. Her favorable opinion of his character mattered little to him because it would change nothing.

She met his gaze. "So, when my background was researched, was there anything about me being worthy of being your bride?"

Kardahl's gaze was drawn to her mouth and his pulse quickened. "There is only one way to answer your question."

"How?"

He cupped her cheek in his palm as he brushed his thumb back and forth over her mouth. "Like this," he said, lowering his head....

Dear Reader,

I've often said that I have an imagination and I know how to use it. As a writer, I've learned that even imagination is limited by the scope of one's experiences, and in mine there's a budget. Not knowing what it's like to own a yacht, a plane or a palace, I dug out a *People* magazine article on rich and famous European royals, because it's difficult to picture a life where money is no object.

I live in Las Vegas, a playground for the rich and famous who join ordinary people from around the world, trying their luck at winning a big jackpot that will change their luck. When you read a romance novel there's no luck involved. The characters are going to find their happy ending, which is why I love these books and always have.

In *The Sheikh's Reluctant Bride* Jessica Sterling wins the lottery of life and love—although she doesn't see it that way when she first finds herself married to international playboy Prince Kardahl Hourani.

I hope you enjoy their story as much as I enjoyed imagining it.

Best wishes,

Teresa Southwick

TERESA SOUTHWICK

The Sheikh's Reluctant Bride

Brothers of Bha Khar

Wedded under the desert sun!

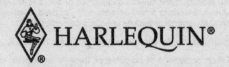

HARLEQUIN®

TORONTO • NEW YORK • LONDON
AMSTERDAM • PARIS • SYDNEY • HAMBURG
STOCKHOLM • ATHENS • TOKYO • MILAN • MADRID
PRAGUE • WARSAW • BUDAPEST • AUCKLAND

ISBN-13: 978-0-373-03945-6
ISBN-10:   0-373-03945-X

THE SHEIKH'S RELUCTANT BRIDE

First North American Publication 2007.

Teresa takes a minute to share why she loves sheikh stories....

"As a reader, I love sheikh stories about powerful men who refuse to show weakness and cover their pain with arrogance. The woman who can capture his heart must be strong and spirited, his equal and the one who can bring him to his knees emotionally. When he finally gives in to love, it's an incredibly satisfying moment."

In June comes older brother Malik's story

The Sheikh's Contract Bride

Wedded under the desert sun!

Journey to the dunes of the stunning kingdom of Bha'Khar! Under scorching desert skies and balmy starlit nights, the scene is set for a royal romance between a sheikh and his contract bride!

To Susan Mallery, Maureen Child
and Chris Rimmer—the best plot group ever.

CHAPTER ONE

"FEAR is my friend."

As the plane touched down on Bha'Khar's runway, Jessica Leigh Sterling prayed she spoke the truth. Except the statement was fundamentally flawed. Fearful flyers usually freaked out on takeoff, not so much on touchdown. But nothing about this flight was usual and she'd learned there were lots of ways to be afraid.

This wasn't like when she was a girl and her mother had gotten so sick that Jess had been sent to the state home. This was scary like the hopeless romantic who finds out it might be possible to get what she's wanted her whole life only to find out her dream really is hopeless.

She was afraid it was going to be like that old joke: everyone who has a family, step forward. Not so fast, Jessica. There are people who share your DNA, but they don't want to know you so forget about them helping out if you need a kidney or bone marrow transplant.

Oh God, to be this close to meeting someone who'd known her mother, someone who might care about Jessica because of that connection. Might. But, maybe not. And she was still a little weirded out because the family she'd come to meet lived in a country halfway around the world from California. But the potential benefits trumped fear and, although important, matching kidneys and compatible bone marrow were not an issue, thank goodness. It was the simple things she wanted to know—like where her brown hair and hazel eyes had come from.

And, just this once, couldn't life come down on the side of the hopeless romantic? That's what she was here to find out.

As the plane slowly turned toward a group of buildings, it hit her that this was really Bha'Khar, her mother's country—the country Jess had never known about while Mary Sterling was alive. The mounds of paperwork necessary to make this visit happen had made her eyes cross and—good lord—the king of Bha'Khar had sent an aide to cut through the red tape. Why had her mother kept secret her connection to royalty? Jessica never would have known if an attorney from the Department of Children and Families hadn't contacted her about the letter from her mother that he'd found in her old file.

The King had sent a plane, too. When it stopped,

the captain turned off the Fasten Seat Belt sign and she released hers, then stood, stretching cramped muscles. She'd been told that someone would be here to meet her, but her nerves didn't seem to care. Then the curtains parted in the forward cabin and a tall man in a close-fitting and elegantly tailored navy-blue suit walked toward her. He looked familiar, but no way could she have ever met him.

He looked about thirty and moved with confidence, predatory grace and an air of controlled power. His thick black hair was long enough to scrape the crisp white collar of his dress shirt. The barest suggestion of arrogance mixed with the sensual curve of his mouth and his straight nose flared a little at the nostrils, hinting at a depth of passion that could rock a girl's world. Only a vertical scar on his lip and a crescent-shaped one on his sharp cheekbone marred his male perfection. And mar was the wrong word. If anything, the imperfections enhanced his masculinity.

He stopped in front of her and smiled. "Jessica?"

That smile could start the average woman's world rocking, but she wasn't the average woman. His deep voice and attractive accent made her name sound like a caress.

"I'm Jessica."

"Welcome to Bha'Khar." He took her hand and bent over it.

Along with the plane ride, this was a first. Kids

from the state home didn't grow up and rub shoulders with the sort of men who kissed women's hands. It made her feel awkward and ill at ease. Like that first night after being taken from her mother's hospital room to share a room with other girls who had no one. All the hopeless, empty, scary feelings came back in a rush.

Then his soft lips grazed her knuckles and the touch unleashed other feelings that had nothing to do with anxiety and everything to do with awareness.

"Th-thank you," she said.

Dark brown eyes assessed her. "Please forgive my boldness, but I am compelled to say that I did not expect that you would be so lovely."

English might be his second language, but certainly he was fluent in flattery. Could flirtation be far behind?

"Thank you," she said again.

It was the polite response to the man who'd probably been sent to take her to her relatives. But every single instinct she possessed elevated from alert-level-orange to run-don't-walk-away red. Suspicion was the by-product of a childhood spent watching alcohol destroy her mother's body as surely as the string of two-timing men through her life had destroyed her spirit. Jessica had learned to spot a player by the time she was ten years old and this guy was definitely a player.

But that wasn't her problem. He was probably another of the king's aides and she was nothing more than his job. After he connected her with family, his work would be done.

"I trust your journey was pleasant?" He continued to hold her hand and for some reason she continued to let him.

Pleasant? She glanced at the plush, customized interior of the royal jet. "There was some turbulence." Her heart had raced then, too. "But mostly the flight was smooth. Although I have nothing to compare it to. This was my first time."

A gleam stole into those dark eyes. "So... You are no longer a virgin—" Two beats later he added, "Flier."

That, too. She'd never slept with a man, either. Many had been willing to be her first, but she'd been unwilling to participate. She didn't believe there was a faithful guy out there, let alone one who could sweep her off her feet. An unfortunate characteristic of the hopeless romantic was the yearning to be swept away, which put her idealistic and rational selves in constant conflict. She wanted a completely romantic meltdown that would prohibit logical thought and just let her *feel*. So far she'd come up empty on all counts.

Although the way her stomach had dropped when he'd kissed her hand made her feel like she was still in the air and the plane hit a downdraft. Imagine if he kissed her for real—on the mouth. Darned if her lips didn't tingle at the thought. This so wasn't the time to abandon logical thinking. What had he just asked? Her journey. Right.

Time to cleanse the virgin remark from the air and turn the conversation to the mundane. Make that nonpersonal because there was nothing ordinary about this guy or the royal jet. "This plane is amazing. It's like a flying living room."

"There is a bedroom as well," he said, suggestion in his tone adding to the gleam in his eyes.

So much for nonpersonal communication. "I noticed."

"You found the bed comfortable?"

More comfortable than the way he made her feel. It was like every nerve ending in her body had received a double dose of adrenaline.

"I found everything perfect."

"Excellent. There is a car waiting. I will escort you to the palace."

"The palace?" She knew her eyes grew wide, and tried to stop, but couldn't, what with her heart pounding so hard.

"Is there somewhere else you wish to go?"

Yes, she wanted to say. And no. "Going to the palace" didn't fit into her frame of reference even after reading her mother's letter. She remembered the handwriting, as familiar as if it were the day's grocery list instead of the last thing her mother had written ten years ago. The words still made her heart hurt. *I know I did everything else wrong, but it wasn't wrong the way I loved you.* Since then, Jess had read the message over and over but still couldn't grasp that she was distantly related to Bha'Khar's royal family.

"I'm sure the palace is fine, but—" Fine? It so wasn't fine. She wasn't a palace kind of person. She was burgers and fries, sweatpants and sneakers.

"But?"

"I was sort of hoping I'd be meeting my family."

"And you will," he promised. "Arrangements are being made. In the meantime, permit me to make you comfortable."

Comfortable? What did that mean? And how could she be comfortable with strangers, however distantly related, who were royalty?

As he started to turn away, she put her hand on his arm and felt the material of his suit jacket. "Wait."

Concern that seemed to be genuine slid into his eyes. "Is there a problem?"

The problem was the material just felt like material to her. It was probably expensive material, but she had no frame of reference for that any more than she did for a palace. Most little girls grew up playing pretend princess, but the fantasy was usually limited to the great gowns and a tiara or two. Not living under the same roof as the king and queen. This was a fear she'd never felt before.

"Maybe it would be better if I stayed at a hotel."

He looked puzzled. "The king and queen would be disappointed."

How did she explain this? "There's a saying in my country—it's better to look stupid than open your mouth and prove it. This is kind of like that."

"I like this saying. But you do not look stupid so I am unclear on your point."

"They're certain to be disappointed in me, but staying at the palace—I'm bound to do something that will let them down for sure," she explained.

He shook his head. "You need only be yourself."

"That's what I'm afraid of."

"There is no cause for fear."

"Yeah, there kind of is. This is a perfect example." She held out a hand indicating the plush plane interior. "I grew up in a run-down, one-bedroom apartment on Stoner Street in Los Angeles. That was until the state of California took over. I wouldn't know a shrimp fork from a forklift."

"You are exaggerating."

"Yes. But you get my point."

"If it becomes necessary for you to know these things, just stay very close to me and follow my lead. I promise to protect you."

She studied the oh-so-sincere expression on his handsome face. "That sounds very much like 'trust me.'"

"Exactly."

"In my country when someone says that it's usually a good idea not to."

"You are most cynical," he commented.

"I have good reasons."

"I look forward to hearing them," he said, probably just being polite.

He smiled, showing off straight white teeth, then he covered her hand with his own, a gesture meant to comfort but brought back the spiraling-plane-sensation.

"The king and queen are looking forward to meeting you, the daughter of their dear friends' daughter, for whom they've been searching so many years."

"They've been searching?" she asked, her gaze jumping to his.

In the letter, her mother had confessed that she'd become pregnant by a married diplomat and ran away because shame prevented her from going to her family. Jess had feared the same family would shun her and to find out they'd been looking gave her hope a double dose of adrenaline.

She smiled up at him. "Thank you—" Had he introduced himself? Was she so caught up in her nerves, skepticism and his charming flirtation that she'd forgotten? "I'm sorry, I don't know your name."

"My apologies. I have been remiss." He bent slightly at the waist. "I am Kardahl, son of King Amahl Hourani of Bha'Khar."

That name sounded familiar. Probably because he was part of the royal family. "So are we related?"

He shook his head. "Your lineage can be traced

back to royalty, but the bloodlines split off over a hundred years ago."

There was no reason to feel relieved about that and yet she was, right up until she realized why the name sounded so familiar. And why she'd thought she'd seen him before. Because she had seen him in print. He was better looking in person. "You're the playboy prince." Did she say that out loud? Oh God, the look on his face told her she did.

His eyes narrowed. "You have been reading the tabloids."

"I don't buy them," she said. It was a minor distinction, but a distinction just the same. "But it's hard not to see them in the grocery store, the beauty salon, the doctor's waiting room."

"You might want to choose a physician who does not patronize disreputable publications," he said.

"I don't have a choice." This was proof that they could be living on different planets. He had no clue about her reality. "My kids go to doctors contracted with the state and we don't get a vote on the publications in the waiting room."

"You have children?" he asked, a flicker of surprise in those dark eyes.

"I've never given birth if that's what you're asking. I'm a social worker and kids in the state's care are my responsibility."

"I see."

"I doubt it. Probably you never had to worry

about medical attention, or your next meal or a roof over your head since you grew up in a palace not a group home." She made a mental note that irritation cancels out fear.

"You would be correct."

Lucky him. "What should I call you? Your Highness? Your Worship?"

"He who rules the universe is my preferred title."

She blinked. "I'm sorry. Were you being funny?"

"Apparently not."

But he smiled, a charming smile that made her want to grab hold of the nearest chair. Another mental note: this playboy had a sense of humor and it packed more punch than his charm. She didn't know whether to be grateful that her player radar was alive, well and functioning with one hundred percent accuracy or unsettled to have proof that she'd inherited from her mother the playboy-magnet gene. The thing was—she wanted to be swept away, but by someone who sincerely wanted *her* and men who were players didn't do sincere.

She'd just confirmed that he was everything she didn't want in a man. Not that he would hit on her. According to those questionable publications, his taste in women ran to models, actresses and world-famous beauties. She was not, not and *so* not.

"My friends and family call me Kardahl," he was saying.

She nodded. "Kardahl it is. I'll just get my bag—"

"It will be taken care of." He rested his hand at the small of her back.

She swore the heat of his fingers seeped through the material of her suit jacket and made her want to melt. Probably that was because he smelled really good. She'd read somewhere that sense of smell was a powerful weapon in the arsenal of seduction. Still, there was the whole willingness thing and he'd just kissed the hand of maybe the only woman on the planet who was immune to his tabloid-worthy charisma.

Kardahl did not miss the chill that slid into Jessica's large hazel eyes when he had introduced himself. Or the way she quite deliberately moved away from his touch now. Given their relationship, her reservations were puzzling.

He held out his hand, indicating that she precede him. "Let us go."

He settled her in the back of the limousine and supervised the removal of her luggage. There were only two pieces, a meager amount of belongings all things considered. It was his experience that women always brought more than necessary and she was moving her entire life. Strange, indeed.

Kardahl slid into the back of the car beside her and met her gaze. The scandal precipitating her arrival was entirely his doing. He'd lost the only woman he would ever love and when he had grown weary of being told life goes on, he had thrown himself into the business of living—with many women. And he was guilty of the abundant yet judicious use of flattery. But he had told *this* woman the truth about being quite lovely. Her sun-streaked brown hair fell past her shoulders, with shorter strands framing a delicate face and cheekbones that revealed her noble heritage. She had also inherited lips that were full, well-formed, and quite frankly, the most kissable mouth he had ever seen.

"Tell me about yourself," he said.

"I'm disappointed."

"You have only to tell me who has done this and I will see that a high price is paid for the transgression."

"Look in the mirror," she said dryly. "Surely you can do better than 'tell me about yourself.' I've heard some of the world's best pickup lines. For instance— 'here I am, what are your other two wishes.' Or, 'do you have a Band-Aid? I scraped my knees when I fell for you.' Or, my personal favorite—'Do you believe in love at first sight? Or should I go out and come in again?'"

"You do not believe that I sincerely wish to know you?"

She slid him an assessing glance. "How's that uber-sincere line working for you?"

The puzzle of Jessica Sterling deepened. Revelation of his identity had altered the obvious female interest he had first recognized when her pulse raced and her hand trembled in his. Gone was the friendly, open woman he had first met. Now he found her prickly. Skeptical. And if he was not mistaken, suspicious. This was a reaction he had never before encountered from a woman. It was remarkably refreshing.

He smiled. "The line works quite well, actually. When I politely and sincerely inquire to know more about a woman, she invariably rewards me with information about herself. Intimate information."

"Okay. I'll play along."

"Play? This is a game?"

"What else?" she asked. "This is you."

He nodded. "Then if you choose to treat it as a game, I will play along, too."

"I figured you would," she said.

"So, if you please, tell me about yourself."

She blew out a long breath. "I was born in Los Angeles, California. My mother died when I was twelve. I grew up in the child welfare system. Went to college and received a degree in social work." She shrugged. "Those are the highlights of my life."

Kardahl did not believe that was so and only now recalled that his father had intended to have Jessica's background investigated. Undoubtedly it had been done, but Kardahl's indifference to the situation had prevented him from reading the report. He regretted that now.

As the car sped smoothly toward the palace, he

looked at her. "I suspect there is more you are not saying."

A frown marred the smooth skin of her forehead, then she turned to look out the window. There was tension in the line of her jaw, the length of her slender neck, the set of her shoulders. Her hands rested in her lap, fingers intertwined, but there was nothing restful about her as she rubbed one thumb over the other.

"There's a lot I'm not saying, but it's not important." Finally she met his gaze. "Tell me about you."

She did not wish to talk about herself, which made him all the more curious. But there was time to learn what he wanted to know. "I am the second in line of succession to the throne of Bha'Khar—"

"The spare heir?"

"Some would say."

"So you're like the equivalent of the vice president in my country."

"I suppose that is true."

"You're so busy keeping women happy all over the world. When do you have time to get ready?"

"For what?"

"To rule the country. If you're called on."

He did have a reputation—some of it deserved, some embellished. But no one knew why he took pains to cultivate it. "I will do my duty should the need arise, but I pray it will not because my brother, Malik, will one day be king."

"Of course. Tell me more."

"What do you wish to know?"

"I wish to know how someone like you who was born with so many advantages and opportunities to do really good things can turn into a self-absorbed pleasure seeker who's only interested in his next romantic conquest."

Her tone was friendly, conversational. And because he liberally used flattery, he recognized it in women. He was accustomed to it. He definitely did not see it now. "You have quite a low opinion of me."

"It's hard not to, what with all the stories printed about you and women who are equally self-absorbed and pleasure seeking."

His emotions had shut down two years ago after burying his beloved Antonia and he almost didn't recognize the prick of anger now. "Do you believe everything you read in those publications?"

"At the very least there has to be a grain of truth or they would be subject to accusations of slander followed by expensive lawsuits. And how many times have denials been issued only to find out the story was true? So, yes, I do believe a lot of what I read." She met his gaze directly. "Although I have to say you look nothing like your pictures."

"The paparazzi are not interested in taking favorable photographs. Their goal is to take infamous ones." And they did not care who they hurt in the pursuit of that goal, he thought bitterly.

"And you certainly give them ample opportunity."

"If you have such a low opinion of me, it begs the question. Why did you agree to come here?"

"You know why. The king's representative promised to make it possible for me to meet my family." She met his gaze. "After that, I'm going back home to my job with the department of social services—important, relevant work. Something you probably wouldn't understand."

"You would be wrong." He was the minister of Finance and Defense. "I am quite social."

She smiled. "No doubt about that, but the services you provide are questionable."

She was making assumptions without knowing him and it was beginning to grate. It was as if she were trying to elicit emotion from him, even if that emotion was negative. If that was her objective, she was destined for more disappointment. The passion he had once felt was big and blazing, an entity with a life of its own and an excitement that had consumed him. When he lost that, he lost everything. He was empty inside. He had learned to go on by embracing that feeling of nothing and Jessica could not do or say anything to make him care.

This was about duty—in his case duty had been helped along by the unfortunate photographs of him with a certain still-married and much divorced actress. With negotiations in progress for Bha'Khar to join other nations in the Global Commerce Union, a scandal in the royal family would not be tolerated. As the public relations minister had pointed out— the only thing the media loved more than a salacious story was a salacious *love* story that included a wedding.

But that was not the real reason her presence in Bha'Khar had been expedited. The woman Kardahl had loved was dead, along with their unborn child and a part of him had died with them. Now one woman was the same as the next. It had ceased to matter to him that the king had chosen his bride when Kardahl was just a boy. His heart had turned to stone.

But his confusion was increasing. What was this about her going back to a job? It would explain her scarcity of luggage, but created more questions.

Kardahl frowned. "One who takes vows so cavalierly should not be so swift to point accusing fingers."

"Vows?" Her smile disappeared. "What are you talking about? What vows?"

"The vows we took by proxy."

Her eyes widened. "I don't understand."

Neither did he. But this he knew for certain. "You are my bride."

CHAPTER TWO

THREE hours ago Jessica had been afraid the family she'd only just found might reject her because she was the result of her mother's out-of-wedlock pregnancy. Now she had bigger things to worry about, like marriage to a man who didn't know the meaning of the words vow, dedication and loyalty.

In his palace suite, she paced back and forth in front of the French doors that opened to a balcony overlooking the Arabian Sea while she waited for him to return and tell her it was all a big mistake. They'd have a laugh, then she could get on with the reason she'd come here.

At least she had a great view for her pacing and his suite wasn't bad, either. Not bad was a gross understatement. It was big. And while she was tempted to explore, she didn't want to lose her way and get caught snooping. What she could see right here was pretty awesome. Celery-green sofas done in a suedelike fabric faced each other in front of a white brick fireplace. Pictures, each with their own lighting, hung on the walls throughout the spacious living and dining rooms. She didn't know a darn thing about art but would bet each one cost more money than she made in a month because they were filled with difficult to identify body parts. And they were difficult to identify because they weren't where they were supposed to be. Kind of like the mess she now found herself in.

How could she be married and not know it? What about the white dress, flowers, rings and vows—preferably of the verbal kind. Her low-heeled pumps clicked on the mosaic tiles in the suite's foyer as she checked the door to make certain it wasn't locked, then peeked outside to see if anyone was standing guard there. No and no, she thought, closing the door.

That didn't mean she wasn't a victim in some bizarre sex slave ring. She'd seen stories. Granted it was far-fetched. When the royal family had taken her under their wing, she'd never suspected another agenda, but what did she know? She thought proxy marriages had gone out with horse-drawn buggies and hoop skirts.

While she was trying to decide whether or not her luggage would slow her down too much when she made a run for it, the door opened and Kardahl joined her in the living room.

"I have news," he said.

She tried to read his expression and when she couldn't, made a hopeful guess. "We're not married."

"On the contrary." He held out a piece of paper. "Is this your signature?"

She took it from him and stared at the familiar scrawl beneath the foreign words. "It looks like mine, but—"

"Were you coerced?" he interrupted.

"No. But I remember a stack of paperwork taller than me and—"

"Not such a very great stack of paperwork then," he interrupted, looking her over from head to toe.

She was going to ignore that. "Not being fluent in the Bha'Kharian language, I couldn't read this. The man who was supposed to be helping me said it was nothing important. That I was simply giving my permission to open records that would unite me with my family."

Kardahl nodded as he took the paper she handed back and set it on the glass-topped coffee table. "In his overzealous desire to serve the king, he may have stretched the truth."

"He lied?"

"Not exactly. Your signature gives your permission to access records, but it also bears witness to your agreement to the marriage by proxy."

"That's absurd. This is 2007. No one gets married by proxy."

"I assure you it is quite real and legal."

As yet, she wasn't outraged to the point where she missed the irony of being this man's bride. Nine out of ten women would be alternately doing the dance of joy and counting their lucky stars. But Kardahl got reluctant woman number ten. But irony worked both ways. She was apparently *legally* married to her worst nightmare. That kicked her outrage into overdrive.

She put her hands on her hips. "How do you know I'm not already married?"

"Do you not think someone would have checked that?"

"I never thought I'd be in a proxy-marriage situation. How did this happen?" she asked, pacing again. "Why did I draw the short straw?" At his blank look she translated, "Why me?"

"Your mother's lineage can be traced back to royalty and there is a long friendship between our families. Many years ago it was decided that her offspring would become the bride of the king's second son—"

"What if she'd had a boy?" Jess demanded.

"But she didn't," he pointed out, far too calmly as his gaze lingered on her breasts. "So when your attorney made inquiries and you were located, plans for the union proceeded."

This was wrong in so many ways, she didn't know where to start. Actually that wasn't entirely accurate. "Did you sign one of those papers, too?"

"Yes."

"Voluntarily?"

"Yes," he answered far too patiently.

The playboy prince signed a marriage agreement without a gun to his head? "Why?"

"It is my destiny. The spare heir is required to marry and produce children."

Since when was he the poster boy for following the rules? "What if I'd never been found?" When he opened his mouth, she held up a finger to stop him. "Don't you dare say 'but you were.'"

The corners of his mouth curved up. "It is not necessary since you have said it for me."

"Then I'll rephrase— What prevented you from getting married before this? If I'd never turned up, would you never have married?"

"A suitable bride would have been selected." He shrugged. "When the time was right."

"So the time was right now? Because I was located?"

"That—and other things." He looked like a naughty little boy caught red-handed.

The expression was cute, she thought, before her outraged self scratched the observation and replaced it. He was no boy. The girly parts of her recognized and responded to his masculinity against her will and better judgment.

"What did you do?" she managed to ask.

"Why do you assume that I am at fault without really knowing me?"

She folded her arms over her chest and looked up. "How can you ask that with a straight face. This is you we're talking about. The whole world knows about your romantic escapades. Of course you did something. What was it this time? I'm sure a woman is involved," she guessed.

"She left her husband, although the separation is not yet legal."

"That would make her a *married* woman. I guess the king wasn't too happy with you."

"Not me so much as it is the pictures of myself and the lady taken with the telephoto lens." He shrugged, but his eyes narrowed. "My father and his advisers made it clear that this was an opportune time to—what is the expression—kill two birds with one stone."

"Squash the scandal and do your duty?"

"Exactly," he agreed.

So the king had one nerve left and Kardahl had gotten on it—and dragged her along with him. She put her hands on her hips. "There's just one problem. I don't want to be married."

"May I ask why?"

"So many reasons, so little time," she said. "And if I did decide to walk down the aisle—and I mean walk down the aisle, not sign a piece of paper and presto you're hitched—you're the last man on the face of the earth I would choose."

Instead of irritation, amusement sparkled in his eyes. "Is that so?"

"Your behavior proves you're not capable of commitment." She waited for his expression to change and when it didn't, she said, "Feel free to deny it and set the record straight. The basis for that opinion comes directly from the tabloids."

"There is no need to deny it. You are correct."

"Then why didn't you refuse to go through with this proxy thing?"

The amusement finally disappeared, replaced by a dark look that made his eyes hard as granite. "It is the price of royal birth. This marriage is about duty."

"That's the thing. There is no marriage because I didn't knowingly give my consent." She never would have given it, especially if she'd known who she was marrying. "In case there's any question, I am not happy about this."

"That is understandable. You have been ill used."

He was agreeing with her again. Why did he keep doing that?

"Come again?"

"You should have been apprised of all the facts of the situation. The aide responsible for this will be severely disciplined."

"That's a start. How severely?" she asked cautiously.

"How severely would you like?"

Good question. How did you chastise someone responsible for marrying you to the kind of man you'd avoided like the stomach flu?

She looked at him. "If the punishment were to fit the crime, he should be forced into a marriage with the last person on the planet he would choose."

"He is already married."

Laughter slid into Kardahl's eyes indicating he got her drift and didn't care that she'd slighted him. Why should he when the world was his playground and all the women in it his adoring toys.

"I see. And does he also have children?" she asked.

"Three."

Ouch. She didn't want to be responsible for the man losing his job when he had a wife and kids depending on him. "Maybe a severe talking to would be enough. Along with a warning not to play with people's lives."

"I will arrange it," he said. He bowed slightly and smiled.

"Don't do that."

"It is a gesture of respect," he explained.

"Not the bow. Don't smile at me."

He tilted his head as he studied her. "You would rather I frown?"

Yes, she thought. For many reasons. Not the least of which was the way his smile made breathing a challenge and threatened her equilibrium. "How can you smile when we still have a big problem? How are you going to get me out of this marriage?"

"It is possible to obtain an annulment," he said.

"Okay," she said nodding. "I'm almost smiling. What do I have to do?"

"You must not consummate the marriage."

This must be hopeless romantic hell. She was discussing sex as if it were a business deal. So much for being swept away. "Okay then, start the paperwork. I promise not to seduce you and I'm quite sure you can't seduce me."

"Are you so very certain?" There was a gleam in his eyes. The glitter of competition, a challenge issued.

"Oh, please. I'm looking for a man who can put his heart and soul into a relationship. You're not that man and we both know it."

"Do we?" He looked at her for a long moment, then shrugged. "If you wish it, I will begin the process of dissolution."

"I wish it very much." Clearly he was being so agreeable because he didn't want to be married. Then a thought struck her. "Is this going to get you in more trouble?"

"Do not worry about me. I will explain to the king and queen."

"There won't be more scandal?" she asked.

"My public relations staff will issue appropriate statements. But—"

"What?"

"If I could prevail upon you to play the part of my wife—only in public," he added, "until any hint of scandal has faded away. You would have my gratitude. And although my family has caused you some distress, they would be forever in your debt as well.

And in the meantime, I will give you every possible assistance in meeting your family."

Family. It's why she'd come halfway around the world. Because she'd had no one after her mother died, she'd always longed to have the problems with relatives that others moaned about. She would cherish interference, being judged and unwanted advice if she gained unconditional love.

"It's a deal," she agreed. "As long as no one expects me to produce children."

His only response was a smile and a look that reminded her of a large hunting cat selecting his prey.

As the limousine drove past the colorful booths of the open marketplace and continued toward the heart of Bha'Khar's capital city, Jessica stared out the window shaking her head.

"Something is not to your liking?" Kardahl asked.

"Everything is fine."

And that was an understatement. True to his promise, he had shown her to her own room and she'd spent the night—alone—in the most beautiful bedroom she'd ever seen with a closet as big as her whole apartment in L.A. The bed was so high, she'd half expected her nose to bleed. The bathroom vanity was marble and all the fixtures were gold. After a pleasant breakfast, Kardahl had told her his staff was contacting her family and while they were waiting for a response he offered to take her on a tour of the city. It was very sweet, but probably part of his scandal-suppressing charade. And she was okay with that.

What saddened her in a soul-deep way was that this lovely, graceful city with its white and pink stucco buildings and red-tile roofs had been her mother's birthplace and Jessica had never known. It was part of who she was and made her feel as if pieces of her heart were missing.

"Tell me what troubles you," he said, his voice deep and gentle.

The gentleness got her. That and the fact that he'd read her so right and wouldn't let her brush him off. "I can't believe that my mother never talked about her country and her family."

"It must have been a bitterly unhappy time for her."

"Why do you say that?" she asked.

He shrugged. "It is a reasonable assumption. One tries to forget unhappy times. Talking of them would simply keep the pain fresh. In addition, the burden would be heavy enough without weighing down a child."

So he thought her mother was protecting her. He looked sincere and it made sense, although she hadn't expected such a depth of understanding from a man with his reputation for superficiality.

She smiled at him. "Whether or not you're right, I find that very comforting." When his cell phone rang, she looked out the window at the Arabian Sea.

The sparkling blue expanse disappeared as they drove down a narrow street with fashionable shops on both sides.

He folded shut his phone and said, "That was my secretary."

He looked at her. "I waited until your arrival to confirm a visit to your family."

"When can I meet them?" she asked eagerly. "I don't know much about them."

"You have two aunts—"

"My mother had two sisters?" Duh. He'd just told her as much. What she'd meant was, she'd always wanted a sister, or a brother. She'd desperately wished for someone so she wouldn't be alone. Her mother had sisters and she'd walked away from that, never looking back. Why?

"One of your aunts," he continued, "is married to the ruler of Bha'Khar's desert people. The other is a doctor who lives in a city to the north of the capital. I have arranged for you to meet them both."

"That would be wonderful." She was almost afraid to ask. "And my grandparents?"

"They are on an extended diplomatic assignment at the request of the foreign service minister. They've been informed of your arrival and will return as soon as possible."

"I see." She sighed.

He frowned. "What is it?"

"I'm disappointed that I have to wait," she

admitted. "I'd hoped to spend as much time as possible getting to know them before I have to return to my job."

"Can you not extend your leave of absence?"

"I suppose I'll have to, but I hate to do that to the kids."

"They are not being cared for while you are gone?"

"It's not that simple. Getting kids to trust when they've lost everyone isn't easy." She knew from personal experience. In fact, she still never let herself believe in anyone with her whole heart. "It's a leave of absence for me, but to them it's one more rejection. One more person who abandoned them."

"They must learn not to put their trust in a single person," he said. "It is a lesson that will serve them well. Would they not be better off without you?"

She shook her head. "Everybody needs somebody sometime. If they don't engage emotionally, they become isolated and antisocial."

"Is not detachment more uncomplicated?"

She stared at him. "This from a man who attaches himself to anything in a skirt—" She pressed her lips together and sighed. "Never mind."

"Do not misunderstand. I have great admiration for your devotion and the conviction that you can make a difference." His tone said it was a waste of time.

"The world would be in sadder shape than it already is if no one tried."

"I wish you luck in your efforts."

This attitude was what she'd expected based on what she'd read about him. And if not for his insight moments ago she never would have questioned it. But she wondered how he could be so understanding and so jaded at the same time.

She was about to ask when she glanced out the window and realized they'd stopped. "Is the tour over?"

His smile was mysterious. "Yes. And now I have a surprise." When the driver opened the door, Kardahl slid out, then held a hand out for her. She took it and he closed his fingers around hers, drawing her to her feet on the sidewalk in front of a dress shop. Then he slipped her hand into the bend of his arm and said, "Come with me."

Inside, the perimeter of the store was lined with women's clothes—dresses, suits, full-length gowns. If one couldn't have a fairy godmother with a magic wand, shopping was the next best thing. But there was nothing magic about her budget and she was pretty sure it wouldn't withstand the prices in this place.

"Why are we here?" she asked.

Before he could answer, a saleswoman appeared, smiling broadly when she recognized Kardahl. "Your Highness, I was delighted when you called. Please give the queen my regards. As you can see, I have canceled all other appointments and closed to the public as you requested. So this is your wife?"

"Jessica," he said.

"She is quite lovely. My congratulations on your marriage."

"Thank you," he said, glancing down at her. "My wife is in need of some clothes. And there is a reception tomorrow night."

"There is—" Jess stopped, not wanting to blow his cover. But it would be helpful if he didn't spring stuff like that on her in public.

The next thing she knew, the woman had whipped out her tape measure and after taking measurements said, "She is a perfect size two. I have some lovely things that will be most flattering to Her Highness."

Jess wasn't anyone's "Highness," but she didn't quite know how to phrase it even if she could persuade someone to listen. Not to mention outing their marriage for the sham it was. The woman bustled around the room plucking a sage-green suit, black silk slacks and several coordinating blouses before disappearing, presumably to a fitting room. When she returned, Kardahl pointed to a slender, black evening gown. "I wish to see her in this."

The saleswoman smiled. "It is fortunate that the gown is her size. And Your Highness has excellent taste."

As well he should, Jess thought. His Highness was a notorious flirt and playboy who no doubt had intimate experience sizing up women as he removed their clothes. The thought made her shiver and that was a problem. Jess's mind was saying no, no, no, while her body grew more curious. And her heart was telling her she'd have to be six feet under to not salivate at the chance to at least try on these clothes. But how could she tell the woman she was wasting her time?

When she disappeared with the evening gown, Jess turned to Kardahl. "Listen up. This isn't necessary. I don't need anything. We both know the annulment is coming. And—"

"And until then, the world will be watching my wife. There is the matter of the reception tomorrow evening." He smiled. "I saw your eyes light up as you looked at everything. It would please me to do this and the least I can do for the inconvenience imposed on you. At least try the things on. The woman would be disappointed if you do not."

"So you're playing the disappointment card again." She sighed. "Is that a royal order?"

"Would you like it to be?"

She sighed. "Yes. It has to be wrong to defy a royal order."

"Indeed," he said.

She heard the smile in his voice as she turned away and left to find the saleswoman. Around the corner was a fitting room with the clothes she recognized hanging on various hooks. Jessica figured she was probably a spineless slug, but what the heck? She was stuck and might as well enjoy the experience.

Everything fit as if made for her and her female

heart was full to bursting at the prospect of wearing such exquisite styles, such delicate, shiny fabrics that rustled when she moved. The saleswoman, Jasmine, bustled in and out, removing items as she brought in more. The black dress Kardahl had picked out was the last thing she tried on.

Jessica looked at herself in the full-length mirror and her eyes went wide. The neck was high and the sleeves long but the soft satin clung to every curve and revealed as much as it concealed. She turned and gasped at the flesh-baring back.

"It is perfect for you." The woman ran her hands over the hips and waist. "His Royal Highness requested only to see you in this."

"He did?"

The woman nodded. "He said to tell you it is a royal order."

The downside of orders were the ones you didn't want to obey. But her choices were to either suck it up, or cause a scene. As she left the dressing room, Jess held the skirt of the gown up to keep from tripping on the long hem. When she walked into the room where Kardahl waited, she held her breath. He stood and took her hand, helping her onto the dais in front of a bank of mirrors before stepping behind her.

Jess could see him in the mirror, the smoldering look in his eyes as his gaze took in every inch of her. Her feet had been on solid ground for twenty-four hours, but her stomach dropped as if she were taking off in the royal jet. The only explanation was emotional drought, she thought. She wasn't used to men looking at her the way he was and it was like setting fire to the dry brush of her romantic heart.

"I don't think this suits me," she said breathlessly.

"It suits me," he said, his voice as deep and appealing as sin. "We will take it with us," he informed the saleswoman.

Jess said nothing because she wouldn't embarrass the royal family in public. But elegant and costly clothes wouldn't change anything. She might have been chosen for a prince, but she wasn't raised as a princess. All she wanted to do was get to know her family, then go back to her life.

By the time she was dressed in her off-the-rack slacks and shirt, the dress was in a protective bag and Kardahl had arranged for the rest of the clothes to be delivered to the palace. When they stepped out of the store, the crowd gathered outside suddenly surged forward, flashbulbs exploding from every direction.

"Who's the lady, Your Highness?" asked one reporter.

"Is she married, Your Highness?"

Someone shoved a microphone in Jessica's face. "How did you and Prince Kardahl meet?"

Without comment, Kardahl pulled her to him, using his body to shield her from the cameras. Then he thrust her into the waiting limousine.

As she struggled to control her hammering heart, Jess looked at Kardahl. The expression of fury on his face was completely and utterly shocking. Something told her this reaction wasn't about unauthorized pictures or unflattering photo angles. This was a deeply emotional response.

She wondered where the easygoing, charming flirt had gone when she didn't want to wonder about him at all.

CHAPTER THREE

How ironic to have a skirmish with the paparazzi only hours before this meeting with the king and queen. Kardahl had once hoped the woman he would be presenting to his parents as his wife would be another, but thanks to his father, that was never to be. Still, the time had come for introductions.

Now he sat beside Jessica on the sofa in his parents' living room. Faline and Amahl Hourani, made the side by side overstuffed chairs look like thrones as they studied their "daughter-in-law." They had once scrutinized the woman of his choice and found her wanting, but tonight they looked pleased. At least someone was, he thought.

His father's dark hair was flecked with gray on the sides, giving him what most thought a distinguished look. Kardahl had no feeling one way or the other. He only knew the king was a rigid and uncompromising man, difficult to please and stubborn. Kardahl would never forgive him for refusing to waive tradition so that he could marry the woman he wanted.

Unlike her husband, his dark-eyed mother would not permit a gray hair to invade her lustrous, shoulder-length hair. For a small woman, she possessed a strength of will and sense of humor that kept her husband both intrigued and in line. At one time, Kardahl had hoped to emulate their relationship. Those hopes had died with his beloved.

"Are you sure you will not join us in a brandy, Jessica?" his mother asked.

"Thank you, no. Coffee is fine." Jessica set her china cup on the saucer resting on the side table.

She was casually dressed in black slacks and a co-ordinating silky black and white blouse. Her hair was pulled back into a loose bun at her nape, with numerous sun-kissed strands escaping the confinement to caress her graceful neck. The scent of her skin filled his head with the fragrance of sunshine and flowers as her shoulder brushed his own. She seemed unaffected by the nearness, but he was not so fortunate.

"I understand you had your first experience with reporters today, my dear," the king was saying.

"Yes, Your Highness."

The king turned a displeased look on him. "How did this happen, Kardahl?"

He had wondered also and made inquiries of his security staff. "It seems there is a site on the Internet where the sighting of a high-profile individual can be posted practically as it is occurring."

Jessica stared at him. "You mean anyone monitoring that site who happened to be in the area could walk up and shake your hand?"

"Yes," he said grimly. "My guess is that the news media monitors the site."

"But that's practically stalking."

"In a free society," the king said, "it is the price we pay. Also part of the cost is minding one's behavior. As Kardahl knows all too well."

Jessica glanced up at him with what looked like sympathy in her eyes, then back to his father. "I can't help feeling responsible. They found him because he surprised me with a detour to the dress shop—"

"You took her to Jasmine's as I suggested?" his mother interrupted.

"I did," he confirmed, sliding his arm along the top of the sofa, then resting his fingers close to Jessica's shoulder.

Until that first meeting on the plane, Kardahl had been annoyed at the turn of events, but had subsequently learned that Jessica was even less pleased than he about the situation. She was an unwilling participant and unprepared for this life. And the look on her face when the paparazzi had besieged him had made him want to protect her. As he had been unable to protect Antonia.

"Those people are predators who feed off others," he commented.

The queen sighed as she shook her head. "The press can be difficult."

"I just wasn't prepared for them," Jessica said. "Up until today the most excitement I ever had shopping was when the clerk forgot to remove one of those security devices and I set off the alarm when I tried to leave the store."

The king smiled indulgently. "My dear, if you would change your mind and stay with Kardahl here in Bha'Khar, you would be given instruction in dealing with the media."

"Probably not by Kardahl," Jessica said, glancing up at him with humor sparkling like jewels in her eyes. "Unless he used himself as a cautionary tale."

His father laughed. "No. I think my son would not be the best instructor." Then he turned serious as he met her gaze. "I urge you to change your mind about the annulment."

"You're very kind—"

"I hear a 'but,'" the king interrupted. "Your grandparents are dear friends. They would be greatly pleased by a real marriage to join our families."

"You're very kind," Jessica said again. "*But,* I'm not royal family material. In spite of the betrothal, circumstances intervened and I wasn't raised to be the wife of a prince."

Kardahl saw her fingers clasp and tighten until the

knuckles turned white as she rubbed one thumb over the other. When he glanced at her face, the tension in her delicate jaw and shadows in her eyes did not escape his notice.

"You would have a staff to help and the queen and I would—"

"Enough." Apparently Kardahl had to protect her from his father as well as the press. He rose. "Jessica has expressed her feelings and I will not permit you to pressure her."

"Kardahl." The queen frowned. "That is no way to speak to your father."

"For the time being she is my wife and in this instance, it is precisely the way. I have promised her a tour of the palace. We are leaving now."

Surprise flickered in Jessica's expression when she looked up. Before she could expose his lie, he held out his hand. "Are you ready?"

"Yes." She put her fingers in his palm and stood up, then smiled at his parents. "Thank you for dinner."

"You are most welcome," his mother said. "We look forward to seeing you at the reception tomorrow evening."

"And you as well, my son." There was anger in the king's order.

"I will be there."

For Jessica. Kardahl led her to the elevator that would take them to the first floor. He was impervious to his father's moods now. Once he had cared, but that ended when the king chose tradition over happiness. If Kardahl had been allowed to marry the woman he wanted, she might still... But that was something he would never know. His fingers clenched into a fist as the rage-fueled powerlessness blazed through him. He had learned it was preferable to the pain.

Jessica looked up at him. "Are you all right?"

"I am fine."

She pointed. "That vein throbbing in your forehead says you're lying."

Instinctively he touched his temple and smiled reluctantly. "Let me rephrase. I will be fine."

"Thanks for coming to my rescue in there, but you didn't need to. Your father didn't upset me. I know he was just trying to help."

"He was attempting to impose his will on you. Tradition is more important to him than anything."

She folded her arms over her chest and stared straight ahead. "I understand that my opinion is flawed because I never had traditions or relatives telling me what to do. But I don't think you appreciate how lucky you are to have a family who cares about you."

When the elevator doors opened, he waited for her to precede him, then pressed the button. "You are correct."

"I'm glad you see that they love you."

He smiled. "Your opinion is flawed."

"Right." She smiled. "Everyone has flaws. We learn to overlook the worst in the people we love. But I got the feeling that there's something going on between you and your father."

Not any longer. "You are mistaken."

She studied him. "No. You were really angry with him and it was more than the fact that he was trying to change my mind about the annulment."

"We disagree about many things."

"I gathered. But it was also clear to me that your parents love you." She held up her hand when he started to say something. "When you've longed for it like I have, you learn to see it in others. So don't even tell me my opinion is flawed."

"I would not dream of it." On the ground floor, they stepped from the elevator onto the marble tile and Kardahl held out his hand. "This way."

At the end of the short hall, he pulled wide a door that opened into the garden and surrounded them with the scent of flowers and warm sultry air. Inside the walls surrounding the extensive palace grounds, strategically placed lights underscored the proud palms, fragrant jasmine and lush greenery.

Eyes wide, Jessica looked around and breathed deeply. "Kardahl, it's beautiful."

"I thought you would like it here. It is where I come when I wish to—"

"Let your testosterone levels return to normal before you put your fist through a wall?"

"Just so," he said, his mouth twitching as a grin threatened.

Kardahl found himself intrigued by his reluctant bride.

It was said that misfortune built integrity and by that measure, he had much character to spare as did she. Although that was just a guess based on what little she had said about her life. She had edited out almost everything, claiming it was unimportant. He had heard the words, but the pain in her eyes and tension in her voice had said she was lying.

"It's perfect," she said, clearly awed. "I wish I could stay here forever."

He watched her wordlessly take in the garden's natural beauty and thought her own natural beauty a pleasing addition to this serene place. She was like a flower in the desert—strong, resilient and unexpectedly lovely.

"You may come here whenever you wish." He took her hand and placed it in the bend of his elbow, leading her down the path that curved through the flourishing plants.

"But I won't be here that long," she reminded him.

"All the more reason to take advantage while you are able."

"Do you appreciate this? Or do you take it for granted? Like your family?"

"Perhaps," he said with a shrug. He did not take

offense at the question because he had finally read the investigator's report on her life and knew for a fact she had left out much, including that the cause of her mother's death was alcohol abuse. "I cannot change my father any more than you could change what happened to your mother."

She pulled away from him and folded her arms protectively over her chest. For many moments she was silent but finally she met his gaze. "What do you know about my mother?"

"Everything."

"How?"

"When you were located, my father had your background researched."

"And our 'marriage' moved forward even though my mother never married anyone, including my father." Her tone was rife with bitter irony. "But she never stopped looking for 'Mr. Right,' even though every time she thought she'd found him, he let her down."

"Yes." The report had been quite thorough.

"And each time she lost a little more of herself."

"That must have been very difficult."

She looked at him and a fierce protectiveness flashed in her eyes cutting through the pain. "When she was really there, she was my best friend. She listened and we talked. And I miss her still."

"I understand."

"No, you don't. How could you? Your family is

alive and well and all living here in this big, beautiful palace with the gorgeous grounds. And you don't appreciate them." She stopped suddenly at the end of the path and pointed. "What's this?"

He glanced at the salmon-colored stucco walls with their stained-glass windows and graceful red-tile roof. The structure had been closed up since before he was born. "This is the harem."

"Really?" Curiosity shimmered in her eyes, replacing the sadness and successfully distracting her. "So this is where the royal men stash their women?"

"Actually, no. There is a dungeon beneath the palace and secret passages—"

"You're joking," she said.

"Yes." He tried the door to the building and found it locked. "The harem has been abandoned for many years. I believe my grandmother delivered an ultimatum to the king who bowed to her wishes."

"Wow. That sounds like a romantic story."

"I do not know." But if it would keep her eyes shining, he would find out the details.

"I wonder—" She peeked through the window.

He moved beside her, leaning a shoulder against the wall. "What do you wonder?"

"What it would be like to live in a harem." She bent from side to side and stood on tiptoe, trying to see through the stained glass. "Waiting for the call to get in the game. When you're chosen."

"It was more than sex," he explained, noting the

blush that pinkened her cheeks. "Years ago it was a necessity to produce many children in order to ensure the line of succession. The infant mortality rate was very high. Now medical advances make it less important."

"And the women of the world are your harem." She met his gaze, daring a contradiction.

He had sought comfort and forgetfulness in the arms of many and achieved it with none. In this, too, her opinion was flawed, but there was no point in correcting her misconception. Her favorable opinion of his character mattered little to him because it would change nothing.

She met his gaze and smiled. "So, when my background was researched, was there anything about me being harem-worthy?"

Kardahl's gaze was drawn to her mouth and his pulse quickened along with his heart. What would those lush lips feel like? Taste like? "There is only one way to answer your question."

"How?"

He straightened, then cupped her cheek in his palm as he brushed his thumb back and forth over her mouth. "Like this," he said, lowering his head.

The lips that could coax a man into sin without uttering a word tasted even more exceptional than they looked. Softness he had expected, but the innocence he sampled ignited his blood like a torch to kerosene. He cradled her face in both hands and tunneled his fingers into her hair, drinking from her mouth yet unable to quench his passion.

He caught her breathy purr of desire on his lips and felt her hand settle on his chest, over his heart. The touch pitched him into a stormy sea of need, tossing in the turbulence of her temptation. This he had not felt for… Lifting his head, he stared at her bewitching, kiss-swollen mouth. Her breathing was uneven, her eyes glazed with an erotic expression he did not believe she knew was there.

"It is time to—" He swallowed and willed indifference into his tone. Dropping his hands as if she had suddenly burned him, he said, "I will take you back inside."

"G-good idea."

Kardahl was careful not to touch her as they walked back. For two years he had lived with the ghosts of what would never be. Since meeting Jessica, the ghosts had receded for a time, which was unexpected. And unfortunate.

He was comfortable with the pain he carried and did not wish for more. He would not add to his burden by caring again and this bewildering attraction made him grateful that his wife wished to pursue an annulment. He had allowed himself to want women, but this woman could be dangerous to the indifference he had so carefully cultivated.

Knowing she would meet the press, Jessica had thought she was prepared for the reception. She'd been wrong. The black designer gown didn't help. The diamond tiara in the upswept hairdo crafted by the queen's personal hairdresser didn't help. And the professionally applied makeup didn't help. The only thing that kept her from full and humiliating retreat was Kardahl's presence beside her.

He looked pretty spectacular in his black tux and snow-white shirt. But she hadn't had time to fully appreciate that either before this command performance when the announcement of her marriage to His Royal Highness Kardahl Hourani had been made. After a silence that hadn't lasted nearly long enough, the press started firing questions. Kardahl had fielded them easily.

"How did you meet?" someone shouted.

"Are female hearts breaking around the world?"

"Are you really settling down?"

That question brought back memories of the harem where the royal men had gone in years past to satisfy needs. Needs she understood a little better after Kardahl's kiss—a kiss that had come dangerously close to sweeping her away. The feel of his muscular body against hers had ignited a yearning she hadn't known was there.

"Where are you from, Princess?"

The called out question jarred her back to the far less pleasant present.

"How do you feel about landing the playboy prince?"

"You make him sound like a fish," she said. The bright lights made her squint and she resisted the urge to raise a hand and shield her eyes from the constant flashes of light. It was blinding; it was disorienting. It was weird not to be able to see who you were answering.

"What do you do?"

"Will you keep working?"

"When are you going to have a baby?"

"Are you already pregnant?"

The personal questions shouted out so indifferently, so publicly, felt like a personal violation. The last one made her gasp as if she'd been slapped.

Kardahl put his arm around her waist and drew her to his side. "Enough. This interview is over."

The next thing she knew, he was escorting her from the room. After he'd guided her through several doors and shut each one after them, the noise finally receded. He took her hand and led her through a set of French doors and outside onto a balcony with a view of the city lights in the distance. Blessed quiet embraced her along with the pleasantly warm night air.

She breathed in deeply. "I take it back."

"What?"

"When I said you wouldn't be the right person to advise me about dealing with the media. I was wrong. That escape was well done."

He bowed slightly. "I am pleased that you approve."

This knight-in-shining-armor impersonation

didn't fit her formed opinion of him. Was it flawed along with her family sensibilities? Her only legacy from her mother was caution toward men. And this man's exploits chronicled in publications around the world had proven that he wouldn't know commitment if it walked up and shook his hand. So was she wrong about that, too? Or was he a heroic rogue? Was that an oxymoron? Or was she simply a moron for giving this situation more thought than it warranted.

She stood on the tiled balcony in a puddle of moonlight. The last time she'd been outside with him alone, he'd kissed her. The memory made her mouth tingle and she needed to say something to take the edge off her tension.

"You're good at handling the press."

"I have had much practice. As a member of the royal family, I was born into the life of public servant. It is my duty to serve the people of Bha'Khar."

"Female people?" she couldn't help asking. Apparently the tension still had an edge. The words popped out before she could stop them. She didn't mean to be abrupt, opinionated and abrasive. She wasn't normally like this. But he, and more to the point his kiss, had brought out the worst in her. Maybe it was her defense mechanism.

With the French doors behind him, he was backlit and his facial expression concealed in shadow. But the statement had barely left her mouth when his body went rigid with tension.

"I am the minister of Finance and Defense." The words were clipped and precise.

"I'm surprised you have the time, what with pursuing women all over the world." There was the legacy of caution rearing its ugly head again.

"Is it so hard for you to believe that I can put my responsibilities before personal pleasure?"

"In a word? Yes."

"Little fool." His tone made her shiver even though the evening was far from cold. "I am not an unfeeling man."

"Then the scandalous photos are misleading? And everything I've read about you is wrong?"

"You should not believe everything you read in anything but an approved interview."

"So, in spite of what they print, you are open to love?"

He slid his hands into the pockets of his tuxedo pants, marring the perfect line of the matching black jacket. When he turned to the side, light from inside revealed the muscle tensing in his jaw. She thought he wasn't going to answer.

"No," he said. "I am not open to love."

She was surprised he would admit it. "Have you ever been in love?"

She hoped her voice was calm because the rest of her was anything but. His answer shouldn't matter to her but she found every one of her senses finely tuned as she waited for his response.

"Yes," he finally bit out. "I have loved. And she is dead."

CHAPTER FOUR

IF THERE had been anything in the press about this, Jessica had missed it, but that wasn't surprising. Between college and part-time jobs, the world went by and she'd missed everything until after graduation. But everything she'd said to him and the raw pain on Kardahl's face now made her feel lower than a slug. Whatever life-form that was, she was worse. Her only defense was that nothing like this had crossed her mind. Death didn't touch the fabulously wealthy and famous.

She realized that was stupid and knew she tended to romanticize. Everyone got sick; fatal diseases didn't discriminate between old and young, rich and poor.

She needed to say something, but all she could think of was, "What happened?"

His jaw was rigid and edgy anger rolled off him in waves. "It was two years ago," he started, his voice even and low and all the more dangerous for its softness. "An accident."

Not an illness? "How?"

"We were chased relentlessly by reporters who wanted a picture, a story, a word that could be made into a story." He walked to the low balcony wall and looked out into the distance where the lights of the city on the coast twinkled brightly. "Antonia was upset that we were followed, as we had taken great pains to be alone. She absolutely insisted the driver attempt to outrun the horde of photographers although both of us tried to calm her. The roads were wet. The car flipped. She died instantly. Unfortunately I did not."

Now it was the lack of anger in his voice that frightened her. She moved beside him and settled her hand on his arm. When he met her gaze, light caught the scars on his lip and cheek. She reached up and started to touch them, but he ducked away.

"Is that how you got those?" she asked.

"What does it matter?"

That would be yes. Oh God. An apology would be in order, but she didn't even know where to start. "Kardahl, I didn't know. If I had, I'd never have brought up such a painful subject. I'm very sorry. Please accept my deepest condolences on the loss of your wife—"

"Not my wife," he bit out, the anger spontaneous and underlining each word.

"But if you loved her—I don't—"

"The king held tightly to tradition and I was betrothed to another."

He'd been betrothed to her, Jessica realized.

She'd stood between him and the woman he'd desperately wanted and couldn't have—now he would never have his Antonia. She felt responsible, which was stupid since she'd known nothing about him, Bha'Khar or the tradition that was responsible for her being duped into this marriage. But the resentment and lingering pain in his eyes told her he wouldn't want to hear any of that.

"I think now I understand the animosity between you and your father. Under the circumstances, why did you agree to go through with the proxy marriage?"

The hard expression in his eyes made her flinch when he turned his gaze on her. "Because it ceased to matter."

As in he disregarded all women equally because he'd cared too much about one. Jessica was shocked and ashamed in equal parts. She'd misjudged him horribly and insulted him to his face even though he'd been unfailingly polite to her. This rage and resentment were emotions he'd kept well hidden.

From her own experience she knew that the bitterest of tears shed over a grave were for words left unsaid or things left undone. What was it that Kardahl had not been able to say or do?

"I have arranged for you to have riding lessons," Kardahl said the morning after the reception.

During breakfast, he was still trying to understand why he had told Jessica of Antonia. Perhaps because Jessica had provoked him. Or he'd grown weary of her low opinion. Either way, she'd caused him to feel something and he did not like it. All the more reason to facilitate the meetings with her family and send her back to America.

He had instructed Jessica to put on jeans, then escorted her from the palace to the extensive equestrian area where he would personally instruct her. They were standing just outside the stable and the mount he'd chosen for her was saddled and waiting by the fence beside them. "Have you any experience with horses?"

"Why do I need to learn to ride?"

"I was under the impression that you wished to meet your family."

She tucked a strand of hair behind her ear. "Call me dense, but I don't see what one has to do with the other."

"You will need to learn basic riding skills if you are to meet your aunt."

"I can hardly wait," she said eagerly. Her joyous expression turned to puzzlement. "But why do I need to learn to ride?"

"The desert wanderers have settled into their summer encampment in the hills. Horseback is the favored mode of transportation."

She took a step back and looked up at him. "Why can't we take the helicopter? You've got one, right?

Your brother was telling me about the royal yacht and I've already seen the plane. Surely there's a chopper in the family."

"There is. But the terrain is too mountainous." He folded his arms over his chest and struggled not to smile. She had a way about her that reduced the monumental to mundane. "So—I must know what you know about horses."

"I've seen them in the movies and on TV. Does that count?" When the animal beside them shook its head and snorted, she laughed and said, "Busted."

But the look of wariness on her face answered his question more completely than her impudent reply. Kardahl watched the sunlight pick out the gold in Jessica's hair.

He decided she was much like that precious metal—gold—there was a richness to her spirit that was only uncovered when one searched deeper.

As she continued to study the horse, she caught her top lip between her teeth. He was unwillingly reminded of the unfamiliar kind of need her kiss had unleashed inside him. It was a weakness he could not repeat. She thought him shallow and unfeeling, but he would prove that he was trustworthy and would not break his promise. Another kiss would sorely test that resolve.

"Only hands-on experience counts," he said and winced.

"Okay. If that's the only way, then point me in the direction of whoever's going to show me what to do."

"I am going to teach you."

"You?"

He could have assigned one of the eminently qualified grooms, but he'd been unwilling to do so. As to his motivation? It was a decision for which he had no answer.

"Yes. I am an expert rider—" When she opened her mouth to say something, he touched his finger to her lips to silence her, and hated himself for wishing to use his mouth instead. "Do not say you have read of my exploits."

"I wasn't going to." The pink on her cheeks made it appear that she was blushing. A decidedly innocent and refreshing reaction. "I was going to say that you've been very generous with your time since I arrived and I'm feeling guilty about that." She looked down at the red dirt where they stood then backed up.

Traces of guilt lingered in her eyes, but he was certain that had more to do with what he'd revealed to her on the balcony last night. That was less important than why he'd revealed the tragedy. Perhaps her uneasiness at the barrage of media curiosity had unleashed his instinct to protect her along with some deeply buried feelings of grief.

He nudged her chin up with his knuckle as he wished to really see into her eyes. "I do not believe it is my time that is the source of your guilt."

"What other reason could there be?" The question was a diversion but couldn't hide the truth.

"Perhaps you feel that you have misjudged me?"

Her gaze skittered away again. "I'll admit that I was wrong in believing you incapable of sincere feeling. But the fact is your name is linked to many women."

So, she still thought him a womanizer. That was good. He had nothing to give any woman and her poor opinion would keep her at arm's length.

"There have been many women," he said. "But now I am married to only one," he reminded her.

"Temporarily."

"Agreed. But for the duration, you will have my undivided attention."

"That's what I was afraid of," she muttered.

"I beg your pardon?"

"I'll show you what I'm made of," she amended.

He smiled. "In return, I will make certain you are prepared for the journey and I will accompany you myself to see that no harm comes to you."

"Again— Don't you have more important things to do?"

"I have made arrangements. Besides, I promised to help you meet with your family. Despite what you have read about me, I am a man of my word."

"Okay." Then she looked at the horse and caught her top lip between her teeth again. "So… Where do we start?"

"As with any relationship, you must begin by making friends."

Her look was wry. "There are so many things I could say, but it would be too easy. I'm holding back."

"A wise decision." He took her hand and placed it on the animal's neck. "Stroke her and let her become accustomed to your touch and your scent."

As Jessica obeyed his command, he observed her small white hand move hypnotically up and down the chestnut nose and neck of the animal. The scent of this woman invaded *his* senses and he was suddenly and acutely aroused.

"If you are ready," he said, wondering if she heard the rasp in his voice, "It is time to mount."

She let out a breath. "Okay."

Fortunately she did not look at him. "Put your left foot in the stirrup, your hand on the saddle. Then push yourself up and swing your right leg over the horse's rump."

Her movements were slow, awkward, and his fingers itched to reach out and help. But he did not— for two reasons. She needed to learn. And the white cotton shirt and worn jeans that hugged her body intrigued him. He did not trust himself to touch her.

When she was securely sitting atop the animal, she smiled down at him. "Mission accomplished."

"Hardly." He laughed as he handed her the reins. "Mission begun."

He explained how to control the horse by right and left movements with the reins. Then he guided the animal into the corral and with a gentle pat on the rump, it started to walk in a circle. As with all beginners, her backside slapped the leather of the saddle as she bounced up and down.

"Grip with your inner thighs to go with the animal's gait."

Her face wore a look of fierce concentration and he knew she was trying to comply. But Kardahl pictured twisted sheets and her legs around him and the vision produced an intense state of sexual frustration. Forcing away the images, he said, "Don't bounce."

"It's not my fault. The horse is bouncing and I'm just going along for the ride. No pun intended," she said breathlessly.

She continued to bobble like a rag doll and he knew the best and fastest way to get his point across was hands on instruction. Against his better judgment, he swung up behind her and put his hands on her thighs. "Press with your inner thighs. Use your legs or your backside will be most unhappy."

"That makes two of us," she snapped. "I'm trying to use my legs."

And he was trying not to picture them around his waist.

He forced himself to focus on the task at hand. Pressing against her, he used his body to help her get the feel of controlling the animal. For the next hour, he tortured himself, feeling her close. Touching her. Smelling the floral scent of her hair. With every ounce of his will, he attempted to douse the fire she started inside him, but was less than successful. That was unfortunate, because he'd given his word that he would not seduce her.

But it had been easy to give his word before he'd begun to want her.

Anger welled up inside him, like it had last night on the balcony. But now he understood why. He'd forced himself to feel nothing for the last two years, and Jessica was changing that.

Kardahl had promised not to touch her and he would keep his word even though her kiss had told him it was possible to have her despite her denial. He would keep his word because he had no wish to hurt her. He would keep his word because fate had taken from him what he cherished most. At night when he closed his eyes, he remembered the sounds—the screech of brakes, the crash and grinding of metal. Antonia's terrified scream—the last sound he ever heard from her.

He had not been able to stop the reeling and rolling vehicle. In the dark he had not been able to find her. He had been able to do nothing to change the fact that he had lost the woman he loved and the child she carried that he had only just begun to love. He never wanted to feel so out of control again and since then had learned to control the only thing he could—his feelings. He ruled them with an iron will because the only way he could be sure he would never go through such agony again was to never again let himself feel.

CHAPTER FIVE

AS HER horse skittered and danced on the mountain trail, Jessica wasn't so much worried about pain in her backside as she was about keeping her backside in the saddle. Riding beside her, Kardahl reined in then reached over and patted her horse's neck as he spoke soothingly. He had worked with her every day for a week and finally pronounced her skills limited, but adequate for the trip.

"You must relax," he said to her. When she opened her mouth to deny it, he simply cocked his head and stared.

"All right. It's my own fault. When you said we'd be there soon, I got excited."

"Your mount senses this and reacted."

"Even though I'm excited in a good way?"

His serious expression turned wry. "She is smart, but incapable of discerning the fine distinctions of your mood. She knows only that you are not relaxed and this makes her afraid."

"She's not the only one."

"I told you that I would let no harm come to you."

His look was ultrasincere, identical to the one he'd worn when he'd first made that promise and insisted he accompany her on this trip. She'd tried to talk him out of it without revealing the real reason she was reluctant for him to come along. She didn't want to spend time with him.

Since he'd told her about losing his love, she could feel her attitude slipping and she was counting on it to defend her against his three-pronged assault: charm, humor and looks. She needed time to reassert her neutrality, but he hadn't given it to her. Because, she realized glancing around the isolation of the mountains, she figured he was using the time, too, time to let the news of his marriage settle in with the press.

She glanced at him beside her, and her heart gave a little lurch. Although she wanted to blame it on the horse, it was all about the dashing figure he cut in the saddle. Sitting tall and proud, he looked every inch a prince of the desert. High polished boots covered his muscular calves. She'd have thought snug riding breeches would make a man look like a sissy, but not this man. And the loose cotton shirt with wide sleeves that caught the wind was buttoned to a vee that revealed just a hint of dark chest hair, making her want to see more. So much for shoring up her attitude.

"I'm not afraid of falling off my horse," she explained. "At least that's not the only thing."

"What else troubles you?"

Scanning the grass and trees of the hills, she wondered at a country with such diversity of terrain. This was so different from the sand and rocks in the desert below. With a security detail discreetly in attendance, they'd driven from the palace as far as possible, then climbed on horses for the part not accessible to even the sturdiest vehicle—or the family helicopter. Now she could see why. The path was narrow and wouldn't accommodate anything wider than the hips of her trusty mood-sensing mount. And of course Kardahl's.

The thing was, in thirty minutes she might get a family, something she'd wanted for as long as she could remember and thought she would never have. Or, they might shun her because she was the result of her mother's affair with a married man. They'd agreed to meet and that boded well, but she knew nothing about her family. Maybe her mother had good reason for running away and never contacting them again. Jess had always wondered and wanted family, but now that there was a chance, if it didn't work out she knew the fall would be bad. A bruised backside was nothing compared to the bruising her soul would take.

"What if they don't like me?" she blurted out. She sounded like a kid and knew her insecurity was showing. And she wished anyone but Kardahl had seen it, but he was the only one here.

He put his hand over hers. "If they don't like you, then they are stupid and the loss is theirs."

The words pushed the lump of emotion from her chest into her throat and she swallowed once. "I'm sorry. Were you being funny?"

"No."

"Just checking." Her voice cracked and she wished he wouldn't be nice. Although, with the exception of that kiss, he'd been unfailingly nice. And she couldn't blame him for her own wicked streak that made her want him to be less polite and give her another chance to kiss him.

She looked away from the sensual curve of his mouth, at the sun descending toward the top of a distant peak. She didn't want him to see that her tension went deeper than humor could hide. She'd already let him see too much and blamed it on the fact that he'd shown her deep feelings of which she hadn't thought him capable. It just made everything more complicated and would have been so much easier if he'd stayed back at the palace like any self-respecting playboy prince.

They rode in silence for a while and when she felt her nerves pull tight again, she decided it was in her best interest to let him take her mind off things so her horse wouldn't spook.

"Tell me about the desert people," she asked.

He glanced over, then back at the path. "They are wanderers."

"Why? If anyone knows the value in putting down roots, it's me."

"Tradition is their roots. Two hundred years ago a son of the king challenged the rightful heir to the throne." He looked at her. "That is when the bloodlines split."

"So there's a rebellious streak in my family tree."

His only answer was a smile that turned her insides to liquid smoke. "The rebel and his followers were turned away and took refuge in the far reaches of the desert, far from the capital. Since then, they have protected Bha'Khar's borders from invading enemies. Now they maintain the customs of their ancestors and live off the land. They raise cattle, sheep and some of the finest horses in the world. To escape the heat and find grazing land for the stock, they take to the mountains as the summer months approach."

"When I was a little girl, my mother told me stories at bedtime, about the mountains and skilled riders. But I thought it was something she made up."

As Jessica watched the sun disappear behind the mountain, she felt a connection. Maybe she'd inherited a little of that skill and it's what made horseback riding come easily to her. The downside of inherited traits were the less positive ones—like attraction to what you knew was bad for you. Like Kardahl, she thought, glancing over as the wind blew his black hair and highlighted the noble brow and strong jaw. He might be capable of deep feeling once. But now he went from woman to woman on a regular basis, just like every man in her mother's life.

But as they reached the top of the mountain and a village came into view, she was awfully grateful for his presence. His brief history of her people had taken her mind off her anxiety. His steady voice and presence had kept her calm when fear washed over her, the same fear she'd felt when her plane landed in Bha'Khar. She looked at him and realized it wasn't the same fear at all because she'd been alone in that plane and she wasn't now.

As they rode into camp, women and children lined the dirt road, smiling shyly. Kardahl reined in his horse when they reached the center of the village. Jess could see now that the buildings were wooden frames, and semipermanent, but the walls were canvas that could be rolled up for easy transport.

By the time her horse stopped, Kardahl had dismounted. When she prepared to slide down, he reached up and lifted her to the ground. The feel of his strong hands as he let her body graze his own sent tingles of awareness arrowing through her and she realized she was feeling a fear like she'd never felt before.

She'd grown up believing she was alone and had come halfway around the world to meet someone who shared her DNA. It was about to happen. Not only had he facilitated this moment, Kardahl hadn't left her alone. And it was wonderful.

Impulsively she threw her arms around his neck in a hug. "Thank you for bringing me."

"Had I known such a sweet reward awaited, I would have increased the pace," he said, pulling her tight against him.

The seductive humor in his voice brought a flush to her cheeks as she stepped out of his sheltering embrace. This was just part of their deal and so far he'd been her sheikh-in-shining-armor. But it wasn't something she could count on; it was a temporary truce. When she was alone again, and there was no doubt in her mind she would be, unlike her mother she wouldn't be devastated—for two important reasons.

Jessica wasn't expecting romance. And she would be the one to walk away.

She turned and saw a woman with dark hair and eyes coming toward them. "Jessica?"

"Yes."

"I am Aminah. Your mother Maram was my older sister. It is my pleasure to meet you." She smiled her mother's smile.

Jess's eyes filled with tears. "I don't have the words to tell you what it means to me to meet you—" Her voice cracked and she pressed a hand over her mouth as emotion swamped her.

Arms enveloped her again, this time maternal. It was her mother's sister holding her and patting her back and hair as she whispered words that were nothing—and everything.

"Do not weep, little one. This is a joyous occasion."

"I know." Jess pulled back a little then hugged her aunt again. After all, she had twenty-three years of hugs to make up for. Beside her, the horses snorted and pawed their hooves across the dirt. She glanced at Kardahl. "This is His Royal Highness Kardahl Hourani. My husband," she added. She met his gaze. "This is my aunt Aminah."

Her insides lit up like a Christmas tree at being able to introduce a family member, other than her mother, for the first time in her life.

Aminah nodded. "Your Highness, welcome."

"Thank you."

"We received word of your impending arrival and my husband regrets that he could not be here to greet you. He is overseeing the birth of a prized foal. It is unexpected and he sends his apologies to you and the niece he is most anxious to meet."

She had an uncle, too, Jess thought. Along with her inner-Christmas tree, she felt like the kid who'd just opened the gift she'd asked Santa for.

"Please come inside. Rest after your journey."

Her aunt turned away and Jess noticed that the dress she wore was a colorful fabric made of interwoven blue and gold strands. Inside the house propane-fueled lanterns illuminated the interior. In the corner, a wooden frame piled with pillows and blankets served as the bed. There were more pillows grouped around a table in the living area and a small wooden table and chairs sat off to the side.

"Please sit," her aunt instructed.

When they did, she poured water into glasses and set out bread and cheese.

Jessica was too excited to eat. "Now that I'm here, I don't know what to say," she admitted.

"Nor I. Although there is much to catch up on."

"Kardahl said that you—my family—searched after my mother left."

She nodded sadly. "That is true. Maram—"

"To me she was Mary," Jess explained. "I'm not sure where the name Sterling came from."

Her aunt looked puzzled. "It was not your father's surname."

"You know him?" Jess asked.

"I know who he was. And that he betrayed my sister's trust." Her aunt sat and took Jess's hands into her own. "Do not feel shame, my niece. There is none for you. Sadly my sister— I wish, as do my parents that she had come to us. But pride prevented it and we cannot change the past." She smiled at Kardahl. "Tradition has found a way and your be-trothed returned. It pleases my family."

"Mine as well," he said.

Jessica couldn't tell what he was thinking, but his tone was polite, although when his gaze collided with hers the gleam there told her he was thinking of their nonconsummation pact. Then she was distracted when her aunt asked questions about her mother and growing up in America. Jess decided to keep the painful details of her mother's illness to herself, but her aunt was distressed about the fact that she'd grown up in a state home.

Her eyes filled with tears. "Had we but known, you would have been brought to your family. That I was not there for you is a regret that I will carry all the days of my life."

"You had no way of knowing," Jess said. But it was as if the good intentions started closing up the hole in her heart. "It's all right."

"It is not. I know how swiftly the years pass and what I have missed. My own children have grown so quickly—"

"I have cousins?"

Her aunt nodded. "Three. All girls."

"I want to meet them."

Her aunt smiled, but it was a little sad. "They are at school in the city. Because we are herders, our life is not permanent and their father and I insist on their receiving a level of education they could not otherwise have if they traveled with us. I miss them terribly."

"What about the school-age children we saw when we rode in?"

"I teach them. But we have not many resources to offer when they become teenagers."

"So you're separated for months?"

"Unfortunately, yes." Her aunt sighed, then shook off her sadness. "But you must be weary from your journey. I will show you and your husband to the place I have prepared for your stay."

Jessica had a bad feeling that it wouldn't be as big as Kardahl's palace suite. In fact it was probably a single room like this. And that would reduce the wide-open spaces to not-so-wide, not-so-open and space? Not so much. She'd appreciated having him there, but hadn't thought through the fact that he would be *there* 24/7.

Jessica looked around the little house, tent, cabin— she didn't know what to call it—where her aunt had left them alone for the night.

"It's a little isolated from the rest of the village," she said.

"We are on our honeymoon," he reminded her. "Your aunt is most considerate."

"I suppose it's not a good idea to clue her in that there won't be any horizontal hokeypokey because of the annulment."

"No," he agreed. "Even as isolated as we are, that kind of information has a way of being given to the press before it is expedient to do so. For such news to get out too soon would be counterproductive to what we are trying to accomplish."

"That's what I thought." She kept her back to him, hoping the dim lantern light hid the flush creeping up her neck into her cheeks. Glancing around at the place that was the mirror image of her aunt's she said, "This is nice."

"Indeed."

Her nerves jumped and twisted at the pleased note in Kardahl's voice. "It's not what you're used to, though," she commented.

"Rumor has it that I am accustomed to many bedrooms."

Jess glanced over her shoulder and couldn't be sure, what with the subdued light, but it looked like he had a gleam in his eyes to go with his pleased tone. What was that about? An expression came to mind—no good deed goes unpunished. The thing was, accompanying her here had been his good deed, so why was she being punished?

She could have spoken up and told her aunt that they weren't really a couple, but several things stopped her. Number one: she wouldn't embarrass Kardahl or his family. Whatever the state of his morals, he'd only been kind and considerate to her. Stalwart was another adjective that came to mind, but there was no point in carrying it too far. Number two: her aunt seemed so pleased that destiny had taken a hand in their betrothal. Jess had just met her. She didn't want to be a self-fulfilling prophecy, as in the family was going to reject her, therefore she should hand them, on a silver platter, a good reason to hate her.

So she was stuck. And when she found herself stuck, her attitude took on some sass.

She walked over to the wooden-frame bed and met his gaze. "How does this compare to all those other bedrooms?"

His direct look said I'll-see-your-sass-and-raise-you. His eyes smoldered as he deliberately let his gaze wander over her. "It has quite a unique charm."

The look, the words made her shiver and attitude abandoned her. She walked over to the table and bent to smell the wildflowers in a metal pitcher. "It is charming. And my aunt clearly went to some trouble."

"The flowers are indeed a nice touch."

The seductive deepening of his voice on the last word made her shiver again and the surge of aware-ness warmed through her, then settled like a glowing coal low in her belly. If he could do that to her body with a single word, imagine what he could if he actually *touched* her.

"We need some ground rules," she said quickly.

"Oh?"

"When bathing or dressing or at such time any clothing is removed or—"

"When you wish privacy," he said, far too calmly.

"Yes. When privacy is required, the other person goes outside."

"Agreed."

"As far as the bed—" She looked at it again. It

was roughly the size of a standard double mattress. "You take it."

He frowned. "Where will you sleep?"

"I'll make a place on the floor."

"I cannot allow that. I will sleep on the floor."

"And I can't let you do that."

He rested his hands on narrow hips and somehow the stance highlighted his wide chest and the unmistakable power in his shoulders. Response to his overwhelming masculinity shimmered through her and it wasn't helpful to this discussion.

"How do you intend to stop me?" he asked

What he meant was that he was bigger, stronger and could make her if he chose.

"Be reasonable, Kardahl."

"Very well. We will share the bed."

"That's not reasonable. That's—"

"What?" he asked, his chin lifting as a challenge slid into his eyes.

She'd been about to say it was crazy. But he would ask her why and she would have to admit it was because she was afraid. And it was a kind of fear she'd never felt before. It was fear of going where she'd never gone before with a man.

She'd always believed she wanted to be swept away. Now she knew she had to put qualifiers on that wish. And she would. Right after he stopped looking at her as if he knew what she looked like naked.

"I was going to say that's a lovely gesture, but you'll be more comfortable if you sleep alone."

"Do not worry about me. I am accustomed to sleeping with a woman beside me."

The flash of his white teeth made her want to blink and she felt like the mouse to his predatory cat. He was toying with her and doing a fine job. Anything he could do she could do better? That would mean a bald-faced lie—telling him that she was accustomed to sleeping with a man beside her. If she continued to protest, the situation would become much ado about nothing meaning it was definitely something. And she didn't want him to know it was something.

She looked at the bed, then forced herself to meet his gaze. "All right. We'll share the bed."

"Excellent."

CHAPTER SIX

"ARE you comfortable?" Kardahl asked.

That all depended on how one defined comfort. She'd never shared a bed with a man before and here she was, flat on her back beside the world's most notorious playboy.

Jess stared up into the darkness and contemplated her answer. She was huddled between Kardahl's back and the canvas wall. He'd turned away and no part of his body touched hers—as agreed. But she could *feel* him. The sound of his even breathing, the wonderful deep voice, the radiating warmth of his skin combined then curled inside her and added up to temptation.

"I'm completely comfortable," she lied.

"And you had adequate privacy when I left you alone?"

Since she was sleeping in her clothes, the mocking note in his voice wasn't lost on her. "Yes."

"The mountains of Bha'Khar turn cold at night."

"I noticed."

"You are warm?"

Oh, yeah. Especially after seeing him strip off his shirt before joining her in the bed. Unlike her, he hadn't required privacy. "I'm perfect," she said.

"I would be agreeable to sharing the warmth of my body should you require it," he offered.

His deep voice oozed phony innocence, yet it still tweaked the knot of temptation inside her. "I don't think that will be necessary."

Underneath the cover, his body gave off heat like a coal-stoked furnace. And that was before factoring in her own fired-up hormones.

"If that changes in the night, you have my permission to move close."

They were three inches apart, not on opposite sides of the room. And if he expected her to make a reciprocal offer, he was doomed to disappointment. "How self-sacrificing of you."

"Indeed."

It had been a long time since Jess had even had a roommate. And before that, when she was in the home, she'd shared a room, but the temporary situation didn't contribute to an atmosphere of trust or sharing feelings in the dark. She'd always felt isolated and alone. Although she didn't feel that way now, it wasn't an entirely happy sensation. Was this feeling of having someone the reason her mother had gone from man to man? Or was it more than that?

"If my body can bring you comfort, it would be my honor to do so."

"You're a prince of a guy."

His laugh was warm and rich, like coffee and chocolate. And his kiss. She'd never slept with a man, but she had been kissed. Although never the way Kardahl had kissed her. And she wanted that feeling again. So much.

The depth of her longing convinced her she couldn't let it happen again.

"Good night, Kardahl."

"Sweet dreams, Jessica."

Kardahl had flattered and flirted his way into many beds and always he had slept deeply and felt rested the next morning. That was not the case after spending the night beside his wife.

It had taken every fragment of his self-control to keep from touching her when she brushed against him or sighed sweetly in her dreams. He had not been fortunate enough to dream since that required actually falling asleep.

After waking beside her, they had gone their separate ways. Jessica had spent the day with her aunt, seeing the village and teaching the children. Kardahl had watched the men and marveled at their way with the horses in training. As he walked toward the tent where he'd been told the school was located, he found himself anxious to see his wife.

He saw her on the dirt path playing ball with a group of children. The sun was bright and a pleasant breeze drifted through the trees. Jessica was wearing a short-sleeved white cotton shirt and jeans. Sun-streaked brown hair danced around her cheeks and her eyes were bright as she laughed. Surely his reaction was the result of too little sleep, but the tight, heavy sensation in the lower part of his body was sudden and intense. He wanted her.

She waved when she saw him and the children grew quiet, their dark eyes wide and shy as they warily watched him come nearer. When he stopped in front of them, the boys and girls scattered.

Jessica's look was teasing. "Way to clear a room, Your Highness."

"That was not my fault."

"They're a little shy," she admitted. "And how was your day, dear?"

He lifted an eyebrow. "I bought a horse."

She looked surprised. "You don't waste any time. Is it for you?"

"No. My brother, Malik, asked me to pick out a suitable animal for his betrothed."

"I hope his bride-to-be can translate the fine print before she signs on the dotted line."

"He is the Crown Prince. There will be no mistakes."

"Famous last words," she teased.

"And how was your day, my sweet?"

Now *she* raised an eyebrow, but did not comment on his use of the endearment. "I spent the day with my aunt in her classroom."

"You are frowning. Did something happen?"

She shook her head. As they strolled along the path, she picked a leaf from a bush and rolled it between her fingers. "But education here is an uphill battle. No pun intended. There aren't enough books for all the children and the situation is fairly primitive. There's no access to computers or any other technology that would supplement education."

"To do that would take money," he agreed.

"In a prosperous country like this, it's inexcusable that they don't have more." The look she leveled at him was taut with accusation. "And that *is* your fault."

"How so?"

"My aunt said that several years ago her people petitioned for the necessary funds to improve education. As the minister of Finance, the appeal went to you and died on your desk."

"I see."

"Do you?" she asked.

Two years ago he had been lost in his own pain and could not clearly recall that time. He had gone through the motions, but his heart had disconnected.

When he did not answer, she said, "These are your people, too. I know their lifestyle makes it a greater challenge, but there must be a way to get technology to them. It's an oil-rich country, but the children are the most precious natural resource. Someone needs to champion them."

He felt the weight of her reproving stare. "Your passion on this particular issue would make you an exceptional champion. It is unfortunate that you are not staying."

He found that was the truth. She was worthy of respect and her spirit and sense of humor were most engaging. She intrigued and delighted him, which meant he had not disconnected from her as completely as he would have liked.

"I wish my visit could be longer," she admitted.

"Then you are not so very sorry you signed on the dotted line in error?"

Her mouth curved up. "I'm still sorry about that, but not that I'm here. I can't tell you how wonderful it is to meet family."

"Your aunt seems like a fine woman."

"She is." Jessica tore the leaf in her fingers to shreds. "I was just afraid that—"

He stepped in front of her on the path and stopped. "What frightened you?" When she looked down, he slid a finger beneath her chin and nudged, forcing her to meet his gaze. "Tell me."

"I—I didn't know whether or not there was strength of will for me to inherit. I was afraid I was destined to be like my mother."

"In what way?" He had made certain to read the

investigative report his father had requisitioned, but did not know to what she referred.

Jessica's eyes turned dark and troubled. "She never married. There was one man after another in her life and each time she believed he was the one who would be her 'happy ending.' Every time it didn't work out, she drank more—more wine, whiskey, vodka—whatever alcohol she could get her hands on—to help her forget. And that made it easier for men to use her. It was a vicious cycle that cut short her life."

Hearing her speak of it made him sad for the child Jessica had been, a little girl alone. "An alcoholic."

She nodded. "They say the tendency is inherited, so I always wondered. She was the only outline I had and that's hard to ignore even though all the books say it's about choices."

If it were all about choices, the woman he loved and the child he would never know would be here now. There was always pain when he thought about them, but he found it a little less now. Maybe because he found himself involved in someone else's pain and the fear of not knowing whether any of her people possessed the strength of character to fight the demons and had passed on that strength to her.

"I did not know your mother, but I know with a great deal of certainty that she was a fine woman."

"How can you be sure?"

He cupped her face in his palms. "If it was not true, she could not have produced a child who grew into such a beautiful, strong woman."

She smiled, a small smile, but it chased a few of the shadows from her eyes. "Thank you for that."

He dropped his hands and stepped back, because he wanted very much to kiss her. "So you do not regret coming here?"

She shook her head. "I could never regret the opportunity to learn about the traditions I always thought were just make-believe, just a part of the bedtime stories my mother told me."

"Traditions are not always a good thing."

"You say that because you haven't known a life without them."

"That is true. But if not for tradition, we would not be married."

"I see what you mean." She slid her hands in her pockets. "That is a problem."

More even than she knew. He had hoped this sojourn in the mountains would decrease his awareness of his wife, but had found it to be just the opposite. He was having a more difficult time resisting the urge to make her his.

"Actually I'm glad you found me," she said.

"Is that so?"

"Yes. We're invited to a welcoming celebration. The whole village will be there and festivities will be commencing at sundown."

He glanced at the sun just disappearing behind a peak. "Now?"

"I guess so," she said, her gaze following his. "Aunt Aminah says that there will be food and dancing and that we should be prepared to be worn-out."

From her mouth to God's ear, Kardahl thought. If he did not find a way to resist her presence beside him in bed, he would be going to the seventh level of hell. His indifference was fading. He knew this because it was more than lust coursing through him. Jessica would agree that if anyone knew the difference, it would be him. And this was distressing because lust was all he wanted to feel for her. It was far less complicated.

Jessica stood beside Kardahl and looked down at her feet, trying to memorize the steps to the traditional Bha'Kharian folk dance. The villagers played the music on guitars, a violin and harmonica, instruments that traveled well and produced a lively tune. In the open area centered among the tents, a big fire was burning. Men, women and children, including toddlers barely walking, sang and danced.

When Jess tried to follow Kardahl's lead in a crossover step and stumbled, she laughed ruefully at herself and shook her head. "I think I have two left feet. This pathetic attempt to dance proves that I should have left them in America."

"As with all physical activities," he said, "it merely takes practice."

All physical activity? What did that mean? Was she reading a significance into those words that he didn't intend? Given his reputation, it was a logical assumption.

"I've had lots of practice waltzing, but this is more like line dancing and I've never been able to get the hang of that."

"Then we will waltz," he said.

The next thing Jess knew, she was in his arms, following his lead in a slow dance. She felt his hand on her back, holding her close but not close enough. The fingers of his other hand curled possessively around hers, but not possessive enough. As their bodies moved and brushed together in time to a tune only they could hear, the dance was intimate—yet not intimate enough.

In his eyes she could see the bonfire flames flickering and snapping and wondered if he saw the same in hers. And whether it was in actuality burning logs or a fire inside them. They had arrived in the mountains twenty-four hours ago and this was the first time her breathing had been affected by the altitude. She prayed that, combined with the exercise of dancing, was the reason drawing air into her lungs became a challenge.

She prayed it had nothing to do with the solid, masculine contours of his body pressed to the feminine parts of hers. She hoped it wasn't the spicy scent of his skin invading her senses, dividing her rational and sensuous selves as he scaled her resolve on the way to conquering it. If he had an ulterior motive, she didn't want to know. If he was up to something, she wouldn't be his willing fool.

She moved out of the circle of his arm, executed a deft twirl, then put her own contemporary moves— as in hip action and footwork—to the music. Everyone clapped, including Kardahl, as he smiled broadly.

"You most definitely do not have two left feet," he assured her, a gleam that had nothing to do with the fire lighting his eyes. "That leaves only practice."

"Right," she said wryly. "About that—"

"Jessica." Her aunt Aminah joined them. "Your Highness," she said, with a slight bow. "I have arranged a surprise for you in your tent."

Jess frowned. "I don't understand."

"It is time for you to retire."

Since she knew her aunt wasn't talking about an end to her productive working years, this had to be about going to bed. "But the party is still going strong. And I'm not tired," she protested.

In the glow from the fire, Aminah's teeth flashed in a wide smile. "That is good. You and your husband are newly married and one needs only to see you in each other's arms to know that you wish to be alone."

"No. We're enjoying spending time with every-one," Jess insisted.

Aminah held up a hand. "Do not feel that you are hurting our feelings. We will not think you rude. It is understandable that you are anxious to spend time only with each other."

"No—"

"It bodes well for the duration of the union," her aunt added.

Jessica looked at Kardahl, willing him to jump in any time and help her out, but he just smiled and she wanted kick him. He was a prince, for crying out loud. All he had to do was issue a proclamation that they were staying at the party and everything would be fine. But he just stood there, giving her no choice.

"Thank you," Jess said.

Kardahl held out his arm. "Come, my sweet."

She put her hand in the bend of his elbow and said through gritted teeth, "You're incorrigible."

He laughed. "How you flatter me."

"It wasn't a compliment," she whispered.

When they were in their tent, Jess planned to tell him what he could do with "his sweet" until she spotted a tub of steaming water in the corner. Beside it was a stool with two towels and there were lighted candles scattered throughout the room.

"This must be the surprise," she said.

He glanced down at her. "From the expression on your face, I would say it is most welcome. If you looked at me in such a way, the matter of consummating our union would not be in question."

Oxygen went missing from her lungs again and she couldn't blame the sensation on the fire stealing it. Clearly her aunt intended for them to use this "surprise" together, but no way would she take off her clothes in front of Kardahl, let alone get into that tiny tub with him naked, too.

"Per our agreement, you have to wait outside." They were far enough from the festivities that there was no way he could be seen by the others. "This comes under the heading 'Private.'"

"As you wish."

When he was this close and there were candles and a steaming tub of water, she couldn't think clearly enough to decide what she wished.

"I'll be quick," she promised.

When his eyes caught fire, there was no question that he wasn't talking about a bath. "That is the difference between us. I would *not* be quick."

But he left her alone and she wasted no time undressing and stepping into the tub, immersing herself up to her shoulders in the warm water. It felt heavenly, almost as good as being in Kardahl's arms. That was a dangerous thought considering his reputation and the fact that to keep their union temporary and uncomplicated she had to stay out of his arms. Before journeying to the mountains with him she would have thought herself too smart to fall under his spell. If not too smart, then too cautious. Jess had vowed not to be like her mother and let men take advantage of her inherited romantic streak. Now here she was, struggling against her own nature.

"Is everything all right?"

Kardahl's voice, just on the other side of the canvas from where she sat naked in a tub, startled her and she jumped. Just a thin material separated them, but since she couldn't see him, she figured he couldn't see her.

"I'm fine," she answered. "How are you?"

"As I cannot bask in the warmth of your presence... Cold," he admitted.

There was that fluent flattery again. Two could play games. She splashed loudly. "The water is perfect. Not too cold. Not too warm. Just right."

"I am pleased."

"Wasn't it nice of my aunt to do this?" she asked.

He laughed, but there was more tension than humor in the sound. "I do not believe this is precisely what she had in mind."

"No? I suppose I could have set her straight. But I didn't figure it was time for that yet."

"Your discretion is appreciated."

"Always happy to oblige."

"Not always," he muttered. "Any time you would care to show off attributes of a more *physical* nature, I would be more than willing to participate."

He *was* incorrigible, but she couldn't help laughing. "If I decide to do that, I promise you'll be the first— To know," she added.

But literally the first. With every ounce of her willpower she had to fight the temptation. If she gave in, there would be no going back, and she wanted a clear exit strategy from this marriage.

"I do not wish to rush you, but the air does get cold in the mountains after dark."

The water was starting to cool off, too. A shame since she was thoroughly enjoying herself and being in control of his discomfort. But he'd been a good sport and a gentleman, which she would never have expected when she'd first met him. She washed quickly, then reached for a towel and let out a screech.

"Oh God—"

"What is wrong?"

The biggest, hairiest spider she'd ever seen in her life was parked on one of the towels. She stood, jumped out of the water, then carefully watched that the creature didn't pounce in her direction as she grabbed the other one and wrapped it around her. She'd barely covered herself when Kardahl rushed in.

"Jessica, what—"

"Bug," she said, waving her finger at it. "Do something."

The insufferable man just smiled indulgently. "It is a harmless spider."

"You are so wrong," she said. "Anything that ugly has to be pretty darn harmful."

"It is more afraid of you than you are of it."

"I sincerely doubt that."

He moved closer and captured it in his bare hands.

"Eww. I can't look." She closed her eyes and heard his footsteps, then the flap of canvas that served as a door. Moments later, she smelled the spicy scent of Kardahl and knew he was right in front of her, close enough for her to reach out and touch him. This time all that stood between them was a flimsy towel.

"It is gone. You are safe," he said.

When she opened her eyes, the smoldering look in his told her she was anything *but* safe.

CHAPTER SEVEN

THIS was another in a long line of firsts. Jessica had never been this close to being naked in front of a man, which didn't even register on the safe scale. No part of Kardahl's body touched hers, yet the look in his eyes made her feel as if he touched her everywhere. His breath stirred the loose hair around her face and his gaze lowered to the spot where she fisted her hand in the towel that barely covered her breasts. His eyes grew darker and his nostrils flared slightly, signaling his leashed passion. Her first impression of him had been right. He was rocking her world, big time.

Things tilted more when he bent his head and oh-so-gently kissed her. The butterfly-soft touch was like an electric jolt to her heart and more effective than a finger in an electrical outlet.

A small step forward brought his body in contact with hers, although her fist and the towel kept him at bay. But he continued kissing her, peppering her lips with soft touches that were like a kaleidoscope of passion, brief glimpses of something unbelievably mind-blowing just out of reach.

There was no way to hide her ragged breathing and she didn't try. She should put a stop to this, but she couldn't manage that, either. She'd thought so much about that kiss in the garden, wanting another, and now her wish was coming true. If there was a God in heaven, this heaven would go on forever. But forever wasn't to be, she thought, when he pulled away. This time when she opened her eyes, she saw that his breathing was uneven, too.

He ran unsteady fingers through his hair. "I do not expect you to believe me, but I did not plan to kiss you."

He was right. She wasn't sure she believed him. But the fact that he stopped kissing her when he had her right where he wanted her would give playboys everywhere a bad name.

"Why did you?" she whispered.

His eyes darkened even more if possible. "I could not help myself."

Very original. "Why did you stop?" That was the burning question.

"My conscience compelled me to. Unless—"

"What?" She gripped the towel tighter.

"It is a woman's prerogative to change her mind."

"About?"

"The consummation of our union." He let out a

long breath. "If you are willing, I would be most agreeable to making this a marriage in the physical sense."

Physical meant kissing and she wanted to do more of that. When he kissed her, the world disappeared. It was him, her and a want that took on a life of its own. But he was talking about more than kissing. Before she could tell him she was agreeable, he stepped back. A chill came over her and without the heat of his body, cold reality set in. If she agreed to consummate the marriage, there would be no going back. She felt like that scared girl whose mother was dying, leaving her no choice but to go with the social worker. She didn't ever again want to be without alternatives.

She shook her head. "I haven't changed my mind. I still want the annulment."

"As you wish." The coolness of his voice made her shiver. He grabbed the other towel beside the tub. "You are still wet. Forgive me. I will leave you to your privacy and bathe in the mountain stream."

The next thing she knew he was gone, she was still wet and colder if possible. Quickly she dried off and dressed in sweats and a T-shirt, then slid into bed. A long time later, she heard footsteps before Kardahl lifted the tent flap and came back inside.

His dark hair was still damp and her fingers tingled with the need to run them through the wavy strands. But that wasn't the biggest challenge to her willpower. His chest was bare, revealing a dusting of dark hair across the broad expanse that tapered over his flat abdomen, disappearing into the waist-band of his cotton pants. She closed her eyes and every muscle in her body tensed as she prepared for her second night sharing a bed with a man.

The lantern went out and she was plunged into darkness, just before he slipped into bed beside her. His arm brushed hers and his cool skin was a contrast to her warm flesh. He smelled like fresh mountain air and powerful male.

"I know you are not asleep," he said, humor in his tone.

"How could you tell?"

"Tension rolls from you like waves on the shore."

She didn't know what to say to that. He'd nailed her. So to speak. "How was your bath?"

"Not as warm as yours."

"Sorry."

"Not as sorry as I."

She thought about that and he was right. The re-alization made her laugh. And the more she tried to stop, the more she couldn't.

"You think that is funny?" he asked, but there was laughter in the tone, followed by the deep rumble of it beside her.

"No, it's not funny." She hesitated a moment before saying, "I'm lying. It's very funny. But I can't believe what a good sport you are about all of this."

"I live to serve," he grumbled. "Playboys are not all bad."

"You'll get no argument from me." And she would never have known without spending time with him, time that had brought her a childhood dream come true. "I can't help thinking about how different my life would have been if I'd met my aunt and uncle sooner."

He put one hand beneath his head. "If they had known of your whereabouts, there is no question that you would have had a home with them in Bha'Khar."

She had to agree. Her reception with the people here in the mountains had been warm and friendly. She couldn't imagine a childhood, an actual carefree growing up without insecurity and fear. It might have been enough to erase the emotional baggage she still carried from her mother's heartbreak, weakness and decline. But she would never know.

"Yeah," she said sadly.

"What troubles you?" he asked sharply.

"I'm not troubled. Not exactly."

He was quiet for several moments, then his deep voice warm as chocolate, cut through the darkness. "Life is not a destination, but a journey. Each of us has a destiny at birth and there are many paths to finding it."

"So you believe in destiny?"

"I believe that fate will find a way. If it were not so, your mother's letter would have remained buried in a lawyer's file forever."

"But it didn't."

"No. The discovery restarted a series of events that were set in motion a long time ago."

"Our marriage."

"Just so. You are living out your destiny—for the time being. And it was your family who set that in motion."

"Yes. And I can hardly wait to meet the rest of them."

"Patience, little one."

Easy for him to say. He'd never had to wonder about his family. Clearly there were issues, but the bad you knew was better than no information at all. She was anxious to meet her other aunt and grand-parents. If not, she'd take her annulment and run. Because every second spent with Kardahl made her more restless and edgy.

He was the first man she'd let close enough to sweep her off her feet, but her hesitation had stopped him.

In her wildest dreams, she'd never expected to be married to an international playboy. When she'd learned about the legal tangle, she'd assumed her contempt for his type would be enough to protect her and never anticipated that she could be wildly at-tracted to someone like him. And it just kept getting stronger. The longer she knew him, the more he tempted her. She'd come frighteningly close to throwing caution and good judgment to the wind.

After watching men use her mother, she'd never thought this could happen to her, but she'd underestimated Kardahl's magnetism. She'd pathetically misjudged her own passion. And the worst of all: she'd gotten used to having him around.

She rolled on her side and turned her back to him. She wouldn't misjudge the situation again. There was a lot to like about her husband, but he had already loved and come right out and told her he wouldn't do it again. At the rate he went through women, he'd proven that he meant what he'd said.

Early the next morning, Kardahl had ordered the horses to be ready for their journey back to the capital. The villagers were gathered for the farewells and he watched Jessica hug several people, including her uncle. She saved her aunt Aminah for last and when she pulled away both women had tears in their eyes. Jessica hesitated a moment, then threw herself into the other woman's arms and hugged her one more time, just a little longer.

"I wish I didn't have to go," she said, taking a step back.

Aminah cupped her niece's face between her palms, then kissed each cheek in turn. "Fate has brought you back to us. We will see each other again soon. In the meantime, know that when you go, my heart goes with you."

"And mine stays with you," Jessica answered.

Her aunt smiled, then met his gaze. "You are a prince of the royal blood and my niece's husband. My parents chose you to care for the granddaughter they loved even before she was born. I entreat you to take this responsibility most seriously and hold it in the highest regard."

When he glanced at Jessica, he did not miss the guilty expression on her face. Now was not the time to make known their temporary arrangement. He nodded solemnly. "Consider it done."

Aminah smiled sadly. "Knowing she will be safe makes it easier for me to let her go. Thank you, Your Highness."

He held the stirrup and steadied Jessica's horse as she mounted, then handed her the reins. After he swung into his own saddle, they turned toward the path down the mountain.

Jessica glanced over her shoulder. "Goodbye—"

Kardahl heard the catch in her voice and glanced over. She was looking back, waving, smiling though her lips trembled and the sheen of tears glistened in her eyes. Her reluctance to leave tugged at him, but he did not share it. His relief that their time in the mountains was over could not be measured. One more night tortured by Jessica's nearness while he was shackled by his vow not to touch her would be more test than his self-control could endure.

There was an innocence about her that he found far too appealing, but he was troubled by the sense that it kept her passion prisoner. He had felt it in her kiss and did not wish to risk another opportunity to find out he was correct. That would break his vow and in the grand scheme of things it would change nothing. He would not care again. He could not.

His spirit grew less burdened the farther down the mountain they traveled. The sky above was blue and cloudless. Hawks, with their wings spread wide to catch downdrafts of air, floated above them. His horse and hers were well-behaved and surefooted. Life was good.

Until he glanced at Jessica's face. One look told him there was more on her mind than a bittersweet farewell to the family she'd just found.

"You are uncharacteristically quiet," he began.

"Is that your way of saying I have a big mouth?"

"Absolutely not." As he watched the corners of her mouth turn up in a smile, the knot of need he had not left on the mountain tightened within him. "Let me rephrase the question. What is on your mind?"

"Is it that obvious?"

"Yes. I believe it is more than the sadness of saying goodbye."

"You're right."

And that surprised him. He was not in the habit of deciphering a woman's mood. Since losing his beloved, he'd immersed himself in the complicated task of bringing Bha'Khar into the world order as a financial force to be reckoned with. Between his work and a series of forgettable women who brought relief to his body but none to his spirit, he'd managed to put aside his pain for long periods of time.

But he was beginning to realize that Jessica was not the latest in a string of unremarkable women. She was a woman whose moods he was coming to recognize without effort. Something was troubling her now and he wished to know the source of her agitation.

She sighed. "Aunt Aminah misses her daughters and I feel as if I'm abandoning her, too."

"Her children will be home soon."

"For a visit," Jessica said. "Children shouldn't have to leave their parents at such a young age to receive an education."

"It has been that way for many years," he explained.

"So if it ain't broke, don't fix it? That doesn't make it right. It's not broken, but it could be better. Traditions are good, but sometimes they need shaking up."

"The people who dwell in the desert have chosen this way of life."

"Oh? Like I chose a mother who wanted so desperately to be loved that the bottom of a liquor bottle was the only safe place when she couldn't find it? Or the way you chose to be born into a family who picks out your bride?"

It was a circumstance he had once railed against, then it ceased to matter at all. But learning about

Jessica was making everything change, a fact that was becoming disturbing.

He rested his palm on his thigh, then met her gaze as their horses meandered down the trail. "What is your point?"

"I don't know." She sighed and looked away, shaking her head. "I guess I'm trying to reconcile two such extreme ways of life. You grew up surrounded by luxury. The desert people don't have a permanent roof over their heads."

"Your words sound like an accusation. But it would be idiotic to try to defend myself against the material benefits I enjoy. Regardless of how it looks to the outside world, my life is far from perfect."

Her gaze slid to his. "It must have been difficult losing someone you loved."

"Just so."

"And it would be glib and callous of me to say snap out of it. But fate put you in a situation of enviable advantages and with that comes great responsibility."

"Duty," he agreed.

"As in serving the people of Bha'Khar. *All* the people. Including the ones who alternate homes in the desert and the mountains. You admit you had advantages and one assumes those included an education?"

"Indeed."

"Possibly tutors who came to you?"

He could see where this was going and could only be grateful she had chosen a career in social work instead of the legal profession. She had backed him into a corner and made him feel the need to explain. "I excelled in studies and was at the top of my class in college, up to and including a master's degree in business."

As she studied him, her body swayed from side to side while her horse picked its way carefully over the stones in the path. Her hazel eyes were fervent with what she believed in her heart.

"And what have you done with that exemplary education?" she challenged.

"I am working to ensure Bha'Khar's financial power in the global community."

"What about the community closer to home?"

"Your people," he confirmed.

"My people," she agreed. "I never thought I'd be able to say that. I didn't think I had 'people.' Now that I know about them, I can't turn my back. And I don't see how you can, either."

"I am not."

She sighed. "I know technology has made the world smaller. In the big picture, it's important for the country of Bha'Khar to be a political player. But people make up the country and their needs are vital. People like Aunt Aminah who doesn't get to see her children as much as she'd like because she knows it's important for them to get an education and they have to do that within the existing educational system."

"Education is the key to everything," he agreed.

"But you said yourself that learning could be brought to the high school level without the kids leaving home. All it takes is money and someone who cares."

That was the problem. In the general sense, he was concerned about his people. But the passion had been ripped from his life and he did not wish to resurrect it. "You care. If you wished to discontinue your pursuit of the annulment, you could stay and sponsor the cause."

"I can't stay." She glanced at him and her eyes were troubled. "But you're the money guy. You're in a position to get things done in a hurry." She stared at him and something she saw in his face made her frown. "If you want to."

"It is not as simple as you make it sound."

"It never is."

The trail narrowed and forced them to ride single file. In truth, he was relieved. She was uncompromising, single-minded in championing a cause. Her passion shamed him. She had been orphaned at an early age, yet still truly believed the world could be a better place. He had grown up knowing the price of his advantaged lifestyle was a responsibility to his people. Then fate took the light from his life and he became jaded, disconnected.

Jessica would be an asset to the man persistent enough to chip away at the defenses she had built up. She deserved someone worthy of her and he was not that man.

She put her heart into life and there was no life left in his heart.

CHAPTER EIGHT

JESSICA cradled a cup of coffee in her hands as she leaned against the low wall on the balcony outside her palace bedroom. The silk nightgown and robe were soft against her skin and the most luxurious sleepwear she'd ever worn—and very different from her clothing in the mountains. Staring out at the crystal clear blue water on the coast, she realized that the contrast between the Bha'Kharian lifestyles and terrain was as wide as the sea she was looking at. Fear had receded after meeting her aunt. One hurdle behind her, two to go.

She hoped it was only two. This morning she was troubled. One would have thought she'd have slept better all alone in her comfortable palace bed, but one would have been wrong. She and Kardahl had spent the last two days practically joined at the hip. He'd seen more of her—inside and out—than any man ever had. She'd spent two nights in his bed with the seductive masculine scent of his skin curling inside her. Surely the fact that she missed him was rooted in habit and nothing deeper.

Her feelings had been far less complicated when she'd thought him too shallow to care for anyone but himself. Finding out he'd cared too much was a shock that had gone straight to her heart.

A noise behind her made the hair at her nape prickle and her pulse jump. The familiar zap to the heart told her who was there but she turned to confirm.

"Kardahl," she said. His name came out just above a whisper and the worst part was she couldn't seem to help it.

"Good morning."

He smiled and it affected her like a sweeping martial arts movement that knocked her legs out from under her. Or maybe not just the smile, but the total package. He was wearing jeans, boots and a long-sleeved white cotton shirt with the sleeves rolled to just below the elbow. She'd seen him in suits, a tux and riding attire, but this was the first time she'd seen him dressed this way. It was just as good as all the other looks—maybe not quite as outstanding as shirtless, but darn close. What annoyed her most was that he appeared exceptionally well rested.

His gaze took in her appearance, from the top of her tousled hair to the tips of her red-painted toes—and everything in between. This balcony was shielded from the public and she hadn't thought about putting on clothes before walking outside. When a gleam slid into Kardahl's eyes, liquid warmth trickled through her and settled low in her belly.

This awareness had to be about spending so much time together. The joined-at-the-hip thing had to stop.

"You slept well?" he asked.

"Fine," she lied. "Never better."

"I am glad."

"You?"

"I missed you beside me."

He was lying. He had to be. "It was only two nights."

"But they were memorable nights," he said, flashing his white teeth.

For what didn't happen? Or what almost happened? "I guess you're not used to being in bed with a woman and actually sleeping."

"Just so."

"It was memorable for me, too," she said. Because he was the first time she'd actually been tempted to give herself to a man. "I've been thinking, Kardahl—"

"A dangerous prospect."

"Are you being funny?"

"Yes."

"Just checking." She couldn't help smiling. "You must have better things to do than tagalong with me on this family quest. Aunt Aminah told me her sister is a doctor in the northern city of Akaba. If you could just put a driver at my disposal—"

"That is what I have come to tell you."

"That you're handing me off to a staffer?"

He shook his head. "Your other aunt has responded to the palace inquiries and has sent word that she is eager to meet her niece."

"She is?" Even after her aunt Aminah's warm and loving welcome, Jess needed reassurance.

"She has been told to expect you later today."

"How far is Akaba from here?"

"It is a good distance."

Jess frowned. "Too far to get there today?"

"Not by air."

"I don't want to put anyone to any trouble," she said. "If it's an inconvenience, I'll call her and maybe we can reschedule—"

"It is no inconvenience. The aircraft will be readied."

"I saw that plane. It's pretty big—"

"There is a smaller one—an executive jet," he said, shrugging.

"I guess you can't have too many planes," she said wryly. "Think of all the educational technology that money could provide."

"You are relentless."

"Thank you."

He met her gaze. "We can be in Akaba—"

"We?" She sipped cold coffee as her mind raced. She needed to do this on her own. Not that she didn't appreciate his support. That was the problem. She appreciated it far too much. It was time to cut herself off before the point of no return, which she sensed was dangerously close. "Surely you have better things to do."

One dark eyebrow rose in surprise. "No cynical remark about women?" he asked.

"I guess I deserve that."

After judging him by the standard of tabloid stories, she'd jumped to conclusions. Now she understood why he was never seen with a woman twice. In a weird kind of way, it was sweet that he was protecting them from being hurt. Her mother had been the classic romantic who'd believed she would be the one who could make that elusive alpha male fall in love with her. At least Kardahl didn't lead anyone on.

"I'm sorry, Kardahl." Jess met his gaze. "I don't think I've ever apologized for misjudging you."

"I accept your apology." He looked at the Rolex watch on his wrist. "The plane is being prepared. If you can be ready in an hour, I will fly you to Akaba—"

"You?"

"Yes." His gaze narrowed. "You have apologized once already. Take care with your words."

She winced. He was right. She'd been about to say something snarky, like when had he had time to learn. The thing was, the question was still relevant. He was busy overseeing the quickly expanding economy of Bha'Khar.

"I was just wondering," she said, struggling for diplomacy, "what with all your responsibilities as the minister of Finance, when did you have time to learn, let alone practice?"

"When I was ignoring the needs of my people," he explained.

"Are you being funny again?"

His reply was a shrug. "There has been adequate opportunity to hone my skill on this aircraft. If you believe anything, believe this— I would never put your life at risk."

"It never occurred to me that you would. The thing is, I don't want to keep you from more important matters."

"Right now you are what matters most."

No one had ever put her first. Not ever. So how did she tell him she didn't want to be his priority at all let alone on top? That she needed physical distance to get her balance back.

"Look, Kardahl, it's not that I don't appreciate everything you've done for me, but—"

"Are you attempting to get rid of me?" He folded his arms over the chest she'd seen naked. "Do I make you nervous?"

Yes, she wanted to say, but a thousand horses couldn't drag the information out of her. "Of course not. It's just that you're a man with a public duty and I'm on a personal mission. I just don't want to bother you."

"Correct me if I am wrong, but the sooner you fulfill this personal mission, the sooner you can return to the children in your care. Is this not so?"

Most people would have said it was no bother whether or not it was the truth. He hadn't and the hopeless romantic in her went to the place where she wanted to know if she *did* bother him, the same way he bothered her.

"Yes. I do want to get back to work," she admitted. If they were on opposite sides of the world he couldn't bother her.

"Then I am at your service. I will fly you to Akaba. And I promise that I will let no harm come to you."

There was a point where you just had to give in gracefully and this was it. "Okay."

After that she only needed to see her grandparents before returning home. The thought should have brought comfort, but not so much. And it wasn't life and limb she was worried about. It was her heart. One by one his flaws were disappearing. He was dashing. He was kind. On top of that, he could fly a corporate jet.

Was there anything he couldn't do?

Yeah. He couldn't care for her and the more time she spent with him, the more it mattered.

Kardahl shut down the jet's engines, as always, grateful that the trip had been without incident. And yet, somehow it had felt eventful. He could only attribute that to Jessica. Had he been alone, he would not have been tempted by her voice, her scent and her shapely curves.

He could have made arrangements for someone else to accompany her, as she'd suggested, but he could not. She was his wife—for the moment. But duty only explained part of his motivation. Until the annulment severed their ties, she would be a paparazzi target. He wished only to protect her. But there were ways to do that without becoming personally involved and he was at a loss to explain why he had ignored them.

After unbuckling their seat belts, he left the cockpit and pressed the red knob that released the air from the door seal. Then he pushed down on a lever that freed the stairs for gravity to lower them. After descending, he escorted Jessica to the waiting limousine and handed her inside, sliding in after her. Instantly she folded her hands in her lap and rubbed one thumb over the other.

Kardahl put his hand over hers to still the movement. "Do not be nervous."

She jumped, as if she'd been lost in her own thoughts. But her familiar defensive spirit was evident in her gaze. "That's easy for you to say."

"Actually it is." He smiled at her surprised look. "And before you ask, I was being funny. At least I was making an attempt."

"You could jog in a circle and squawk like a chicken—"

"On the contrary, I could *not* do that."

"Now that's funny," she said, laughing.

He was pleased to see her smile, even though it increased the ever-present temptation to touch his lips to hers. His growing attraction for her continued to be a puzzle. She was not the most beautiful woman he had ever seen. She did not go out of her way to flatter him. And she did not want to share his bed. He could only credit his obsession with her as a challenge to unlock the passion she kept hidden. What stopped him was the risk that he would reveal the heart he had locked away.

"Your aunt will be most pleased to know you. Why do you doubt it?"

"If you'd grown up without anyone, you wouldn't take it for granted, either."

"Perhaps."

And there was probably a great deal of truth in what she said. Since nothing he could say would reassure her, he didn't try. He simply took her hand in his and laced her fingers with his own until they reached Akaba Medical Center where her aunt was the chief of staff. As the car pulled smoothly to a stop in front, he saw the crowd gathered. Word of their visit preceded them and the security detail he had sent ahead had called in uniformed law enforcement officers for backup.

Kardahl looked at her. "I am not pleased to add to your burden, but doubtlessly you have already noticed that reporters are gathered."

"Yeah."

"I feared this might happen. The announcement of our marriage was made, followed by our disappearance for several days. That tends to whet the press's appetite for more."

"I can see why they would be curious." She blew out a long breath. "Let's get this over with."

As they got out of the car, Kardahl felt the crowd move forward as a single entity. He put his arm around Jessica as bodyguards and police surrounded them while they mounted the steps leading to the automatic double doors at the entrance. The click of camera shutters was like the angry buzz of insects as reporters shouted out questions, none of which could be heard.

He would have hustled her into the building, but she turned unexpectedly to face the press.

"I'll answer a couple of questions," she said.

"Are you going to have a baby?"

"Not today."

"Are you pregnant, Your Highness?" someone else shouted, putting a finer point on the inquiry to pin her down.

She laughed and glanced up at him with the absurdity of the question shining in her eyes. "No."

"There's a rumor that you and the prince are having trouble conceiving."

"Not true," she said.

Only because they had not yet tried. And it was not for lack of desire, he thought.

"Are you here because of fertility issues?" someone else asked.

"Why would you think that?" she shot back.

"You've come all this way to Akaba to keep it quiet."

"Also not true. And before you ask, Kardahl and I are not ill. We're here at the Medical Center to visit my aunt, Dr. Janan Fahrani."

"Are you trying to have a baby right away?"

"We haven't talked about it." Jessica smiled enigmatically. "Now, if you'll excuse us, I'm anxious to see my aunt."

She turned away and ignored the relentless media who continued to toss out questions until the automatic doors closed and the quiet, cool marble floors and walls of the hospital lobby embraced them.

Kardahl stopped and looked down at her. "Why did you do that? We could have simply ignored them."

She shrugged. "A split second decision. Gut instinct, I guess. It occurred to me that it's human nature to want what you can't have. If we continue to dodge their questions, everything becomes so much bigger. If you stand and face it, get it over with, it takes away the power. I'm not running away."

Like Antonia, he thought. Her anger at being the prey of the media had incited the tragic series of events that cost her life. It had all spun out of control so quickly. If only he could go back...

Just then, a dark-haired woman in her late forties approached. The embroidery on the breast of her white lab coat read, Janan Fahrani, M.D.

She glanced at both of them but her eager gaze rested on Jessica as she smiled. "I cannot tell you how very pleased I am to meet my sister's child."

"And I'm happier than I can tell you to meet my mother's sister. You look so much like her—" Jessica's voice cracked and she pressed a hand over her mouth.

The other woman opened her arms and Jessica moved into them as the two embraced.

"I met Aunt Aminah," she said, pulling back after a long moment.

"How is my sister and her family?"

"Fine. She misses her daughters," she answered glancing up at him. "I'm sorry. This is His Royal Highness Kardahl Hourani—"

"Your husband. I have seen the news reports of your marriage."

He held out his hand. "It is a pleasure, Doctor."

"The pleasure is mine, Your Highness." She slid her fingers into his. "I apologize that I could not meet you in the capital. My work is demanding. I regret that you had to come all this way."

Jessica smiled. "It was no problem. Kardahl has a plane and he knows how to use it."

Her aunt laughed. "Still, it was good of you to bring her to me."

"It *was* good of him." Jessica smiled and when she met his gaze, there was warm affection in her eyes.

He liked it when she looked at him that way and could too easily grow accustomed to seeing that winsome expression on her face. "Would you still think me good if I told you I was showing off for my bride?"

"I doubt it was just that," the doctor said. She looked at her niece. "I have spoken with my parents and they wanted me to tell you that they are most anxious to meet you and will be home soon. Their schedule of meetings with foreign dignitaries could not be called off, not even for something so important as meeting their granddaughter."

Jessica swallowed hard. "I've been told they searched all these years for my mother. She changed her name, which is probably why the search was unsuccessful."

Janan sighed. "I wish it could have been different, but we cannot alter what has been. We can only be grateful for what is now. And I am most grateful that you have come."

"Since we are here," he said, "would you be so kind as to show us around the facility?"

Her black eyes glowed with pride. "It would be my pleasure."

For the next hour Jessica's aunt took them through Radiology, Cardiology, Surgery, Respiratory and Outpatient Services. She showed them the building where various research studies were being conducted, with revenue spent on promising cancer drugs and diabetes treatments.

As they were walking down the hall, Janan announced, "I have saved the best for last."

She pressed a square metal pad on the wall and the double doors opened automatically. On the left was a large window. Behind it was an open room with rows and rows of newborns and nurses attending to the ones in most need of attention, a fact revealed by their red-faced crying.

"This is the newborn nursery," the doctor explained.

Jessica moved close to the glass and smiled as she stared beyond it. "They're so sweet."

"Our most precious natural resource," her aunt agreed.

"I said that to Kardahl once," Jessica said. "They're just too precious for words. Don't you think so, Kardahl?"

He moved beside her and saw the infants, some squirming and flailing tiny fists. Others sleeping the sleep of the innocent. He barely heard Jessica's words as pain punched through him, and it was like none he had ever known. He had never let himself picture his son or daughter as a living, breathing child. Now he knew why. He had not wanted to think about the fragile life lost, the dreams and deeds that were never to be.

Until this moment he had been successful in

burying this part of his grief but now it sat like a stone on his chest. He could not breathe.

Without a word, he turned and walked away.

CHAPTER NINE

"KARDAHL! Wait."

"I wish to be alone."

"What is it? What's wrong?" Too stunned to move at first, Jessica stared at his broad back for several moments before running after him. When she caught up at the elevator, a brief view of his dark expression put fear in her heart as the doors whispered shut.

"I don't know what's wrong with him," she said to her aunt who had followed. There must be something wrong because just a glimpse of the stark misery on his face convinced her there was something terribly not right.

She pushed the down button. "I have to go after him."

"I have seen that look before," her aunt said.

"What do you mean?" she asked, turning. "You've seen Kardahl before?"

"Not him specifically. The expression. Pain. Loss.

As a doctor, I use my skill and knowledge and everything I have for my patients. But sometimes there is nothing that can be done. And I have to relay this information to the family that their loved one is beyond help." She met Jess's gaze. "He had the look of one who has heard, but has not yet let go."

Jess jabbed the elevator button, as if that would make it come faster. "I have to go after him," she said again. "He shouldn't be alone."

"It is what he wants."

Jess turned on her. "That's what he said, but it's not what he really wants. He lost someone he loved very much. So did I. When my mother died, I was all alone in the world.

Her aunt looked stricken. "Jessica, we did not know—"

"I'm not blaming you. I'm just saying I know how alone feels. Then I came to Bha'Khar and Kardahl has been here for me."

"Of course. He is your husband. You care for him. That is obvious."

Obvious that she cared? Jess hoped that wasn't true. Although she knew it was hard not to care for a man who had been there for her practically from the moment she'd arrived in his country—her country. His support had given her confidence and smoothed the way for meeting her family. Whether he knew it or not, he needed someone now and she wouldn't abandon him.

"He is my husband, Aunt Janan. And I must go to him."

Her aunt nodded. "Go. We will see each other again soon."

Jess hugged her tightly for several moments, then released her and stepped into the elevator.

Jessica paced the penthouse suite at the Ritz-Carlton Akaba. Kardahl had given instructions for her to be brought here but he was missing and she was getting frantic for him to return. If she'd had any idea where to look, she would have, but she knew nothing about the city or where he would go.

Hours of this waiting was driving her crazy with worry. In her work she saw kids like herself who'd lost everything. She'd seen desperation and loneliness mixed with gut-wrenching grief. And she'd recognized it again in the soul-deep sorrow in Kardahl's eyes. Where did a desperate man go? What would he do to outrun whatever demons chased him?

She walked out on the balcony that overlooked the cosmopolitan high-rises that made up the skyline of this bustling city. Far below there was traffic noise. She heard the occasional horn honking and the screech of brakes. The sun had gone down and still there had been no word from Kardahl. Apprehension knotted inside her and squeezed out hunger and every other need but the one to know he was safe.

How could she do anything until she knew where he was, how he was and what was wrong?

Instinct told her this was about something more than losing the love of his life. He'd told her about that and she'd been almost certain that afterward the shadows had lifted from him.

Back inside the suite she paced into the marble-tiled foyer with the circular table and vase filled with red roses. She stood on tiptoe to peek through the security peephole, hoping he would be there, disappointed when there was no sign.

She wandered back through the living room, glancing at the elegant floral love seats, rich dark wood tables and the graceful dining room set with the matching breakfront. In the bedroom, a plasma screen TV was mounted on the wall across from a king-size four-poster bed. As a kid, she'd always longed for pretty clothes and plush surroundings as if lack of it was all that was wrong with her life. Now she had things but everything was wrong. Nothing could erase the worry gnawing away at her. And she realized the finest material things in the world wouldn't have made a difference while she waited all those long nights for her mother.

It wouldn't have eased the anxiety of wondering whether or not her mother would come home at all, or in what condition. It wouldn't have helped when her mother was drunk or when the man she'd thought would love her had let her down again and Jess held her while she cried. It wouldn't...

She heard the door open and close and relief broke through the worry gripping her. Hurrying into the living area, she saw Kardahl lower himself to the love seat. Lines of weariness carved grooves on either side of his nose and mouth. He scrubbed both hands over his face as he let out a deep, sad sigh.

She didn't know why the sight of those innocent babies had triggered this reaction in him, but every instinct she had urged her to comfort him, touch him, let him know he wasn't alone.

She sat down beside him and put her hand on his arm. "Kardahl, what is it?"

He shrugged her off. "I do not wish to speak of it."

"Tough." She touched him again and her determination got his attention.

"Leave me."

"No." She put her arms around his shoulders and rested her head against his cheek. Her hair caught on the stubble as she nuzzled him. "You don't have to talk. You just need to know I'm here for you. I'm not going anywhere."

He turned his head, meeting her gaze with surprise in his own.

"Jessica—" Her name, a whisper on his lips, was a plea for something she didn't understand.

She touched her mouth to his and felt his conflict, his reluctance to take the comfort she offered, but she wouldn't be discouraged. She deepened the kiss and his shoulders tensed, his breathing grew faster, and the groan that sounded in his throat came from somewhere deep down inside him.

He gathered her onto his lap and wrapped his arms around her, burying his face in her neck. He held her for what seemed an eternity before cupping her cheek in his palm and capturing her mouth with his own. Need crested through her on a wave of heat that scorched rational thought and turned it to ashes.

She couldn't kiss him hard enough, deep enough, or get enough air into her lungs. She pressed her breasts to his chest, straining to get closer.

The next thing she knew, Kardahl stood with her in his strong arms and walked into the bedroom. Settling a knee on the mattress, he placed her in the center of the bed with exquisite gentleness.

"I want you." His voice was warm and soft and seductive as black velvet.

He stretched out beside her and undid the buttons on her blouse. Looking his fill at her virginal-white cotton bra, he leaned close and peppered kisses over her neck. Then he parted the sides of her shirt and pressed his mouth between her breasts, tracing her cleavage with his tongue. It was like a jolt of electricity that zapped her from head to toe and made her fingertips tingle.

And she knew. This was what she'd been waiting for—to be swept away by desire, to feel such passion that nothing else on earth mattered but being with this man.

"I want you," she answered, meeting his gaze before wrapping her arms tightly around him.

Rational thought slipped away as her senses took over and reveled in touching and being touched.

If one could be damned to hell twice, Kardahl knew it would still not be sufficient punishment for what he had done. Not only had he broken his promise not to touch his wife, but he had taken her virginity. How was it possible that she had never been with a man? She was so beautiful yet she had come to him pure as the driven snow and he had callously stolen her innocence.

Mesmerized by the rust-colored evidence on the twisted sheets, he damned himself in four languages. He truly was the bastard prince—every bit the rogue and scoundrel the tabloids portrayed him to be. A better man would not have savored the feel of her bare flesh pressed to his as he had held her in his arms through a night that had been far too short. A better man wouldn't want her again, but Jessica had told him more than once that he was not a better man.

He whirled at the sound of the bathroom door opening. Steam from her shower followed Jessica into the room. The perfect body he had memorized every inch of the night before was swallowed by a thick, white terry-cloth robe. Her still-wet hair hung straight around her small face, a face naturally beautiful and free of cosmetics.

When she noticed him watching, she smiled and the look was like an arrow to his heart—an arrow comprised of passionate intensity with a sharp tip of guilt. She was spirited and generous as well as smart and beautiful. Had he but known she had never been with a man he would have...

"Why did you not tell me you were a virgin?" he demanded, putting emphasis on the past tense.

Her hands, in the act of drying her hair, instantly stilled. When she met his gaze, her smile wavered, then disappeared. "Some men would think it was a good thing. You make it sound like a disorder. I promise it's not contagious."

"That is not— You twist my words." He ran his fingers through his hair, struggling with what to say. He had never faced such a situation. "Why did you not say something before it was too late?"

He remembered wanting her more than his next breath, needing to be inside her. He had never felt such passion, and he knew it had been fueled by her simple and unsullied desire, an innocence he now understood. But there had been a moment after entering her, the briefest of seconds after her gasp of discomfort that he had thought was passion. Awareness of her virginal barrier had penetrated his desire-fogged brain, but he failed to grasp the significance in time.

"Too late?" she repeated. "That implies regret. I suppose a good deal more experience on my part would be required to achieve your accustomed standards."

"That is not what I meant—"

"I have to tell you as standards go, it was all a bit disappointing for me. I'm having a little trouble understanding what all the fuss is about."

How did he tell her what she had given him was a most precious gift? She was right. Most men, unless they were complete idiots, would be giddy with joy and probably feeling a healthy dose of pride at being her first. But it was so much more complicated than that.

Kardahl saw the hurt in her eyes and knew he was handling this badly, almost as badly as he had handled her last night. But that was not completely his fault.

"With pertinent information, there are things a man can do to make the first time easier for a woman, more satisfying. If you had told me—"

"So you're saying we have to work on our communication." She dropped her arm and let the towel dangle from her fingers. Her full lips pressed together into a straight line. "Right back at you."

"I beg your pardon?"

"You have some explaining to do, too."

"I do not understand."

"Yesterday— Why did you walk out of the hospital without a word?"

"I do not wish to speak of it."

She tapped her full lips with a finger. "See, that's the thing about communication. It works both ways."

"Your meaning?"

"I didn't wish to speak of the fact that I'd never slept with a man, and yet somehow we just talked about it."

"We did not. You never told me why I was so honored to be the first."

"An honor?" She turned away and settled the wet hand towel on the bathroom doorknob. "Just now, you didn't act honored. However, you're changing the subject. Why did you walk out of the hospital when we saw the babies?"

He closed his eyes as a vision of new life flashed into his mind. Then he felt Jessica's hand on his arm.

"What about the babies?"

"No—"

"You need to talk about it, Kardahl."

"Why?" he demanded. "What is the point of re-membering what you can do nothing about?"

"You can't change it," she agreed. "But if you don't deal with heartbreak, the pain becomes like a festering wound. You need to let out the poison. Talk. Air out everything. Eventually healing happens."

"A wound this deep will not heal."

"You won't know unless you try," she pleaded.

He turned away and went to the window, watching the sun's rays peek over the top of a jagged mountain. "Antonia was pregnant."

Several moments of stunned silence followed before she said, "She was carrying your baby?"

"Yes."

"Did your family know?" she asked.

He shook his head. "I was going to tell them. Then— There was no need."

"Oh God. You didn't just lose the love of your life. You lost your child, too."

"She was just starting the second trimester." He recalled putting his hand on her belly, feeling the subtle changes in her body brought about by the life their love had created. "The child was real to me. That night, the night of the accident, we were discussing our marriage."

"The prospect of going against tradition?"

"I did not care about that." He turned, his chest knotting at the sympathy in her eyes. "And after losing them, I only wished to never care again."

He was seen with women all the time, but never let anyone into his heart. Until Jessica, he had been successful in that endeavor, but she was making him feel again. That did not mean the behavior was to be encouraged and he would not. Caring was a pathway to pain.

"Kardahl, I don't know what to say. I'm so terribly sorry."

"It is in the past."

"Right. If you believe that, then you're lying to yourself. The look on your face when you saw the babies—" She pressed a hand to her chest. "It broke my heart. And when you left so suddenly— I was worried about you."

"I did not mean to distress you."

"That's not what I meant. I was concerned about you—"

When she touched him, he pulled away because he so badly wanted to pull her into his arms. Last night he had found comfort with her as he had no one else. She was making him want to forget his promise and let the tenderness he felt bloom. The sooner she completed her family obligations, the sooner she could go back to America, which would be best for both of them.

Unfortunately consummating their marriage would make the process of ending it more difficult. He did not wish to think about the personal cost and the longer he knew her, the more certain he was that there *would* be a personal cost.

"There is a concern, but it is not so much about me. It is about us. And what we are going to do now. We have consummated our marriage."

"I noticed." Her cheeks flushed pink.

"Then you realize that there is now a problem with the annulment."

Her eyes widened. "Oh. I forgot all about that."

Until this moment, he had as well but could not help being pleased that he was not alone in the over-whelming passion, that he had driven everything but making love from her mind. It had consumed him, a force of nature, like trying to walk through a cyclone.

"What are we going to do?" she asked. She walked outside, to the low wall and leaned her elbows on it, staring out at the rising sun as it made the shadows in the valley disappear. "I guess we'll have to get a divorce, then."

"The legalities will be a bit more complicated."

"If you're talking about alimony or anything like that, let me assure you I don't want or expect anything. I'll be grateful forever that you were here for me in one of the most emotional and difficult times of my life. That's priceless. So I don't see why it has to be complicated if it's what we both want. Neither of us will contest it—"

"What if there is a child?"

She went completely still, then turned to look at him. "No way."

"It was my fault. I did not once think about doing anything to prevent conception."

"It was just once," she whispered.

"That is enough." Even as the words left his mouth, something inside was telling him that once would not be enough with Jessica.

"Of course. I knew that. It's just—" She shook her head, then rubbed shaking fingers over her forehead. "I can't believe it. I'm the perfect example of the idiot woman who doesn't believe she could get pregnant the first time."

"So—"

"So," she echoed.

"If there is a child—"

"No." She straightened away from the wall and met his gaze, her own filled with fear, shock and disbelief. And something else unrecognizable. "There is no child. Fate would not be so cruel."

CHAPTER TEN

A WEEK LATER, as the limousine drove through the city to the outskirts where her grandparents lived, Jessica pressed a hand to her flat abdomen and prayed that she'd spoken the truth to Kardahl and right now she was feeling nerves. It was too soon to know if a baby was on the way.

That didn't mean she was opposed to the idea of children someday. Just that she'd tried so hard not to make the same mistakes her mother had. As far as Jess could tell, the only one she hadn't made was being married the first and only time she'd had sex.

Before she had a baby, she wanted to be in love with the father. Hopeless romantics wanted to be in love period. But while she'd waited these few days for her grandparents' return, Kardahl had been conspicuously absent and that was probably a good thing. She hadn't been completely truthful when she'd told him sex was a little disappointing.

After the first minor discomfort receded, she'd

seen the potential. And the fuss? She'd thought a lot about his comment that there were things a man could do to make it more satisfying for a woman. Her skin tingled and her breasts tightened at the thought of how lovely those things might be. And that was why his absence had been a relief. She didn't trust herself not to fall into his bed again.

She'd also had lots of time to analyze her situation. Jess had grown up without a father's influence on her life, without a father's unconditional love to shelter her. She didn't know anything else and had come to terms with that.

However, it was one thing not to know a father's affection and never miss it, but quite another to grow up wondering why your father can't love you at all. She knew that Kardahl could never love her and she could deal with it. She was a grown up. But she couldn't stand watching him not love her child.

The most frustrating part was that she couldn't even blame him. Not after the tragedy of losing the woman he loved and his unborn child along with her. It was so much easier when she thought him a shallow cad. Now she felt just the opposite and had come to respect him very much. As the big car drove through the security gates and the palatial white stucco house with red-tiled roof came into view, Jess missed his solid, comforting presence.

All her life she'd wanted a grandmother and grandfather who would spoil her rotten and she was about to get her wish. At least to meet them. The spoiling rotten part wasn't as important now as it had been when she was ten. She was nervous, but not nearly as much as when she'd met her aunts. Kardahl's presence had gotten her through and the void left by his absence today was so big it scared her. How could his impact on her life have grown so large in such a short time?

When Antonia was alive he'd been ready to throw tradition out the window. He'd only involved himself in their arranged marriage because love didn't matter to him anymore. But he mattered to her so much more than she'd ever thought possible.

The car moved smoothly up the driveway and stopped in front of the house. An archway with tall, square columns shaded the double doors with their intricate stained-glass design. She'd barely stepped out when one of the doors opened and an older couple came out. Jess's heart pounded as she walked up the stairs.

The woman was a combination of Aminah, Janan and her own mother, Maram. But Jess felt the pieces of her soul come together when she recognized her own brown hair and hazel eyes—eyes shimmering with unshed tears.

"Grandmother—"

As with her two aunts, the older woman wordlessly opened her arms and Jess moved into her embrace. A sensation of peace settled over her and when she was released, her grandfather pulled her to him for a hug.

"I am Esam," he said, holding her at arm's length to study her. "And this is Leena. Welcome, dear child."

"Thank you." She smiled at each of them. "All my life I've dreamed of a meeting like this."

"Our prayers have been answered," the older man said simply.

Her grandmother nodded and slipped an arm around her waist. "Come inside."

The spacious interior was cool and serene. The foyer was covered in stone tiles that stopped at twin curved staircases leading to the upper floor. In the living room, she was settled on a plush white corner group across from a wall of French doors that opened onto a patio and a view of the jagged mountain peaks in the distance. Her grandmother brought a tray with a pitcher, glasses and a plate of sugar cookies and set it on the mahogany coffee table. How cool was this, she thought.

"Tell us about yourself." The older woman handed her a tumbler of ice cold lemonade.

"I don't know where to start."

"Start at the beginning," her grandfather suggested, taking a seat beside her.

She was surrounded by love and felt it with every fiber of her being. Taking a deep breath, she said, "I was born December 2 in a county hospital in Los Angeles."

She told them a version of the truth that edited out the bad parts. But when she related being taken to the state home and growing up with other kids who didn't have family, her grandmother took her hand -and nestled it between her own warm wrinkled ones.

"If only we had known—" Her grandmother sighed, shaking her head.

"Tell me about my mother, before I was born," she said.

"Maram was a headstrong girl," Leena began. "Too beautiful for her own good. Stubborn. Sweet."

"She was our best and brightest," Esam added.

Jess looked at each of them. "But Aunt Janan is a doctor. Aunt Aminah is married to the leader of the desert people. My mother—"

"Ran away." Her grandfather's eyes were sad, a sorrow that went very deep. "She was our youngest, our shining jewel. So beautiful."

"Yes. We still miss her terribly." Her grandmother met her gaze, studying her. "You look very much like her."

Jessica wondered if the resemblance ended with looks and she hoped she wasn't destined to repeat her mother's mistakes.

"Tell us about our Maram. After she left. What happened to her?" Leena asked.

Jess didn't want to tell them the whole ugly truth. Not yet. "She was a good mother. Every night when she tucked me in bed, she told me stories of a faraway kingdom called Bha'Khar and handsome princes and beautiful princesses. I thought she'd just made it up." She smiled at the older couple. "But she got sick, and kept getting worse. Social Services took me away because she wasn't strong enough to care for me. I loved her very much and still miss her."

Esam's mouth trembled, and he pressed his lips tightly together. When he was under control once more, he said, "Let us speak no more about the painful past. Tell us of your impressions of Bha'Khar."

"What your grandfather means is that we would like to know about Prince Kardahl, your husband."

"Yeah, about that—"

"We were in Washington, D.C. when we saw news coverage of the palace reception when the announcement of your marriage was made public," her grandfather explained. "You make a handsome couple. I think you looked happy."

Was that hope she heard in his voice? "I understand you and the king are responsible for the betrothal between Kardahl and myself."

"Yes. The king is a dear friend. We felt it was advantageous to join our families through marriage."

"So you and the king were playing Cupid?" she teased.

He sighed. "It did not work out precisely as we planned. Children have a way of—"

"Doing their own thing?" she suggested.

"Just so."

"But fate has a way of stepping in and righting things," Leena said. "You found your way back to Bha'Khar and the family who loves you. Prince Kardahl is your husband and finally settled down, to the relief of his parents *and*, I suspect, the minister of Public Relations. He simply needed a good reason to stop his high jinks and tomfoolery. He will be a good and devoted husband. All is as it should be."

Not so much, Jess thought. She didn't want to spoil this perfect first meeting by telling them that she and Kardahl had agreed to stay married to take the heat off his "high jinks" while she met her family. After that, she was going back to America, although the means of dissolving said marriage was now a big question mark since they had consummated the union. Looking at the older couple, she decided that was too much information for the brand-new relationship they were beginning. She was simply going to enjoy them.

And she did. Jess spent all afternoon listening to stories of her mother's childhood. She learned about her aunts and cousins and toured her grandparents lovely home and soaked up the attention they lavished on her. But there was a state dinner at the palace and she was still playing the part of devoted bride, albeit reluctantly.

She stood. "I'm afraid it's time for me to go."

"So soon?" Leena looked genuinely disappointed. "But you'll be back, yes?"

"Yes." But Jess knew it would be to say goodbye, and the thought made her chest tight.

With her between them, they walked her to the door. She looked from one to the other. "This day has been a wish come true and every bit as wonderful as I dreamed it would be."

Leena's eyes filled. "For us as well, little one. And the first of many visits."

"You must come back soon," her grandfather agreed. "Your grandmother—Leena—her name means tender. In translation, Esam means safeguard. For all these many years we have been deprived of the opportunity to live up to our names with our granddaughter. We have much time to make up with you. If there is anything you need, you have only to ask and we will make it happen."

With a lump the size of Bha'Khar in her throat, Jessica didn't trust herself to speak. She just hugged them both as hard as she could and found it was more gratifying than any words could be.

As the car pulled away, she looked back and waved. She was no longer alone in the world. She had family. And they had offered to do anything for her. But even the world's most doting grandparents couldn't make it so that she wasn't falling in love with Kardahl.

"Kardahl, we need to talk."

He was just pouring himself a brandy from the

decanter on the bar tucked into the corner of the living room and thought how perfect Jessica's timing was, because he would no doubt need the drink. Those words coming from a woman never induced peace of mind in a man.

"Do we?"

He took a sip of the liquor, then savored the warmth as it slid down his throat. Lifting a hand, he pulled at his black tie, loosening it to let the ends dangle before twisting open the top button of his dress shirt. The state dinner for the Chinese minister of Finance had been long. Only Jessica had been a bright spot in an otherwise tedious evening.

Even now—especially now—the sight of her had need pulsing through him. He knew the jewel-toned green gown covering her from her long graceful neck to her slender ankles was deceptively chaste. The back dipped provocatively low, flirting with the curves of her delightful derriere. He remembered every inch of her soft flesh from that night they had been together.

Kardahl had unburdened his soul and still did not know whether it had been a mistake. But he knew two things—the loss did not weigh so heavily on his heart. And that night had been abundant with intensity, emotion and the satisfaction of learning he had been correct and innocence masked the depths of his wife's passion.

It was later that guilt had settled over him, shame

for his broken vows. But guilt and shame were not enough to keep him from wanting her again. Once had not been enough and doubts hovered at the edge of his mind that he could ever get enough of her. So he had kept his distance but that had done nothing to temper the temptation to touch her and most definitely had not taken the sting out of his need.

She stood in the center of the room, hands clasped, one thumb brushing over the other. A single lamp was lit and he was jealous of the shadows that caressed her lovely face. They were alone and the need to feel her bare skin beneath his hands consumed him. The last thing he wanted to do was talk.

"What is it you wish to say?" he managed to ask.

"I saw my grandparents today."

The inner joy lighting her eyes made him smile. "I can see from your expression that it went well."

She nodded. "They're wonderful. Everything I hoped they would be and more."

He risked moving close enough to crook a knuckle beneath her chin and nudge it up. "Now you look most serious. What troubles you?"

"How much time do you have?" she asked with her characteristic impudence.

"As much as you require."

"Now that I've met them my mother's behavior is even more confusing. I can't imagine why she would run away and never come back."

"I cannot answer that," he said, daring to brush a

finger over her cheek. "No one can. And you probably will never know what was in her mind."

She sighed. "I guess I knew that. It's just they were so warm and welcoming. The house is amazing. And I felt that they would have been there for her whatever she had done, whatever she needed."

"It is not necessary for you to know what was going through your mother's mind. Now that you know your family, the relationship you forge with them from this moment on will be what you make of it."

"I know." She caught the corner of her lip between her teeth. "That's really what I wanted to talk to you about."

"I do not understand."

"I won't have an opportunity to make much of a relationship with them. My goal was to meet them and I've done that. Now I have to find a way to tell them goodbye. It's time for me to go back to America."

The words seized his chest and squeezed the air from his lungs. Before he could stop the feeling, everything inside him cried out against what she had just said. He had known from the beginning that this was the course of things, but… What?

That was before he had come to know her? Before he had come to like her? A time when he had not expected to grow accustomed to her face across from his at the breakfast table. Or when he had saved her from a harmless spider. Or made love to her and yearned for more.

"You cannot go," he blurted out.

"Oh?" Her chin lifted. "I thought we had an agreement."

"It was altered when you came to my bed. By mutual consent," he added

"So what you're saying is that I can't go because I might be carrying a baby?" She turned away from him and started pacing. The sight of her bare back did little to restore rational thought. He had the absurd desire to pull her against him and kiss her until she could not think straight, either.

"A *royal* baby."

She stopped in front of him and looked up, her eyes clouded. "I'm not pregnant."

"You are certain of this?"

"Almost," she said, her gaze sliding away.

"That is unacceptable."

"Right back at you. It's unacceptable to me to give a child to a man who's incapable of loving it."

"That is what you meant when you said that God would not be so cruel."

"Exactly." She blew out a long breath. "You told me that you will never care again. That's not the ideal environment for a child. I should know. My mother loved me, but she loved the bottle more. If and when I have a child, I want it to have unconditional love from both parents and you aren't capable of that. I understand. You went through an unimaginable loss and at first you get points for just breathing in and out when your life stopped. But time has passed and life never started again for you."

Was she right? Was his heart poisoned against a child they might have made? He did not know what to think. He just knew he could not let her go. Not like this. Not yet.

"Jessica—"

"You can't change my mind. There isn't anything you can say—"

"The baby—if there is one—would be in the line of succession to the throne of Bha'Khar. There is a duty to train the child in the ways of royalty should the responsibility of leadership fall to him."

She sighed. "Darn it. That's a low blow."

The miserable expression on her face again made him want to take her in his arms, yet he was the one who had put it there. "I cannot change the circumstances of my own birth and being a prince of the royal blood."

"Yeah, I get that." She folded her arms over her chest. "Okay. You win this round. I'll stay in the country until we know whether or not I'm pregnant."

That was good. The relief pouring through him elevated his mood instantly. "Excellent."

"But I'm moving in with my grandparents. If the press gets wind of it, just tell them I'm taking some quiet time to get to know them. Or come up with a better story. The last thing I want is to cause you or your family trouble."

That was not good. He much preferred that she reside in the palace, near him, but little clue why her close proximity made a difference. Surely it was all about rehabilitating his image, polishing the perceptions of the world in order to facilitate Bha'Khar's acceptance into the ranks of a global economy. But if that were the case, his chest would not feel so tight.

He did not wish her to go. But if she was not pregnant, he did not know how to make her stay.

CHAPTER ELEVEN

If Kardahl had said he cared about her, she would have happily stayed in the palace while they waited to see if she were pregnant, Jessica thought. He didn't even have to tell her he loved her, although she realized that's what she wanted to hear.

She just didn't get him. He'd told her she couldn't go and his eyes blazed in a way that had made her heart pound with something pathetically close to hope and a healthy dose of desire. Then he used the excuse that she might be pregnant as his reason for the order. He made no fuss when she'd said she was going to stay with her grandparents, yet a few hours later, after successfully dodging the press, here he was escorting her there in the limo.

When the big car pulled smoothly into the drive way and stopped in front of the house, Kardahl looked at her, but his blank expression gave nothing away. "Have you discussed this with your grandparents? After all, they are responsible for our betrothal. Would they approve of you leaving your husband and taking shelter with them?"

"My grandfather is my protector. He said so. My grandmother— They said if I needed anything, I should ask." She squeezed the hands clasped in her lap until her knuckles turned white. "And, yes, I called to make sure it was all right if I stayed here."

Anger darkened his eyes to twin black coals. "So," he said, "the fruit does not fall far from the tree."

"What does that mean?"

"Perhaps you are like your mother after all. You are running away."

Without responding, Jessica got out of the car, then climbed the front steps to knock on the door. That turned out not to be necessary as her grandmother opened it instantly, as if she'd been waiting. While the driver carried her luggage into the house, she glanced over her shoulder and saw Kardahl.

Her heart stuttered at the sight of his lean elegant body standing by the open car door. Remembering the exquisite feel of that naked body cradling her own, she shivered with yearning. She had never met anyone like him—kind, supportive, too handsome for his own good. As if all that wasn't enough, he had a pretty decent sense of humor. Quite simply, he was the most wonderful man she'd ever met.

She had her reasons for voluntarily walking away and in no way could it be construed as running.

In a familiar gesture, he ran his fingers through

his thick, dark hair and her heart caught again. How well she'd grown to know him. It surprised her just how much she'd come to rely on him. But a double tragedy had killed his will to reciprocate tender feelings and anything less than a committed relationship was intolerable to her. Now here she was walking into the arms of the family she'd finally found. She'd made the break from him because her heart was breaking. The man she loved could not love her back.

She waved to him, a small gesture and saw him respond before letting her grandmother lead her into the house.

"Now then," the older woman said, "I have requested tea be served in the living room and we can talk."

"Where is my grandfather?"

"He is giving his report on our trip to the Foreign Service minister and will not be home for some time. We will not be disturbed."

Jessica sank into the soft sofa cushions. "Thank you for letting me come here."

"Thank you for turning to us. It is what families are for. But I am curious about why you felt it necessary to leave the prince. Is there a problem?"

Only if she was pregnant. "Kardahl and I have some things to work out and I felt I could do that better if I had some distance."

"I see."

Was she running? Like her mother.

Jess folded her hands in her lap and crossed one thumb over the other. "Why did she run? My mother, I mean. Why didn't she turn to you and my grandfather for help?"

"I do not know for sure."

"You knew her. She was your jewel, your best and brightest. You must have an idea why she didn't feel she could come to you when she found out she was in trouble."

"Pride. Shame." Her grandmother stared sadly out the French doors.

"According to the letter she left me, my father was a diplomatic attaché," Jess confirmed.

The older woman nodded. "Maram met him right here in this house, at an embassy party that your grandfather and I hosted. He was married and far from home. She was young and quite lovely. They flirted and she began to make excuses to see him at the Foreign Ministry office. He made a pretext of coming here to see your grandfather. We knew what was happening and sternly warned her away from him. Esam and I argued with her many times, but our disapproval only seemed to make her want to be with him more."

"So she refused to stop seeing him?"

Leena nodded. "We were beside ourselves with frustration and worry. She was stubborn and so very young."

"And then she got pregnant." Jessica watched the bewilderment turn to pain on her grandmother's face.

"We did not know that at first. She simply disappeared. Then we began to hope it was a child making her too ashamed to come to us and nothing far more sinister."

"Did you go to my father?"

"Of course."

"Cad."

"Yes. Although he had no knowledge of her whereabouts he confirmed that she had come to him and revealed her condition. He told us about his last conversation with Maram and that he'd made it clear he was an ambitious man. He would not leave his wife and risk a scandal."

"Big cad."

"Indeed." Her grandmother's eyes were hard.

Jess smiled at the hostility she exuded, a mother lioness protecting her brood. And Jess was part of the brood. How wonderful it felt to be part of something. She was beyond glad to have someone in her corner. "Did my father stay here in the diplomatic service?"

"He took our daughter from us, we took his profession from him. I'm not proud of it, but…" She shrugged.

"I see." Jess met her gaze. "Considering that, I'm a little surprised you embraced me so warmly. I'm the child of the man who disgraced your daughter."

"She was not without blame." Her grandmother put a comforting hand over hers. "But we never stopped loving her. You are the child of our child and we love you."

Behind the sofa, a low wall separated this room from the dining area and sitting on top were framed photographs. Jess reached over and picked up one of her mother as a young girl.

"Was my mother a hopeless romantic?"

Leena frowned as she thought about the question. "If you mean was she possessed of a soft and romantic heart, I believe the answer is yes. She cared with every part of herself—mind, soul, body. She loved well, but not wisely."

"Do you think I'm like her?"

"I cannot say, as we are just getting to know each other. Clearly you are troubled about something." She smiled, a small upturning of her mouth. "I would have to be very dimwitted not to know that whatever has made your eyes so sad has something to do with His Highness, the prince."

"No wonder my mother couldn't fool you," Jess answered, trying to make light of it.

"I am old, not deaf, dumb and blind."

"You're not old."

"And you are trying to flatter me. I like that in a granddaughter. And I believe it to be sincere, although it is rooted in the fact that you do not wish to discuss what is really bothering you and are attempting to distract me." Her eyes brooked no evasion. "Tell me what is wrong."

"Because I wouldn't stay at the palace Kardahl said that I was running away—like my mother."

"Running from what? Your mother left us because she was embarrassed and feared that she had disgraced her family."

"It's still sad."

"Yes. Although, from the perspective of many years passed, in a way I find her flight oddly comforting. She knew we were hurt and she did not want to see the pain she had caused. What she failed to take into consideration is that hurt heals."

Not in Kardahl's case. He'd made it clear that he would never get over the love he'd lost and the child she'd carried. She put her hand over her abdomen and prayed that they hadn't made a baby.

"You and Kardahl were betrothed and against the odds have found each other and from what I can see, there is a romantic spark."

On her part, not so much his. "I think you're seeing static electricity."

"Joke if it makes you feel better, my dear. But simply because a child shares characteristics of the parent, they are not necessarily predestined to repeat the same mistakes."

"I hope you're right."

"Of course I'm right. Your mother's heart was

stolen by a man who was not free. She fell hope-lessly in love, but it was doomed from the start."

And those words did not make Jessica feel better. Because of Kardahl's past, her love for him had been doomed from the start—just like her mother's. And she wondered which was worse—a series of men who used and abandoned you while you searched for love. Or never trying again because you'd found the one man who'd once loved so well the pain of his loss would keep him from giving his heart ever again.

Her grandmother frowned. "But when you speak of running, are you talking about going back to America?"

"I have a job there," Jess admitted. "Working with children who need me."

"I am certain they do. But consider this—would you be giving to others for all the right reasons?"

"I'm not sure what you mean."

"Just this—I will not pry into your feelings for Prince Kardahl. And you will always have a home here with your grandfather and myself. We under-stand if you decide that your work is the right reason to go back to your home. But before you make that decision, remember what your mother did not—you can leave Bha'Khar, but you will take all your troubles with you."

There was a reason they called it emotional baggage. Jess had come here with very little of it, but if she left now, ten trunks wouldn't be enough to carry all her problems.

When she couldn't hold back the tears a moment longer, her grandmother gathered her into her arms and held her tight. She'd come here looking for family and found it. She hadn't been looking for love, but she'd found that, too.

At least she had someone to hold her while she cried. It was definitely the best and worst of times.

From the moment his secretary told him Jessica called to set up a meeting, Kardahl had been unable to concentrate. It would have been better if the young man had interrupted his conference call. Had he spoken with his wife, far more would have been accomplished this morning. Now he could not get her out of his mind. Truthfully that was not new. It was a condition he had become accustomed to ever since his first sight of her on the royal jet.

The condition had escalated to a state of acute distress in the past several weeks, after he had left Jessica with her grandmother. His suite seemed too big, too empty without her there. But how could that be? It was not as if her petite presence took up so very much space. He leaned back in his office chair and stared at a computer screen that no longer interested him. Nothing held his attention unless it included thoughts of his wife.

In truth, the size of her form, lovely and curvaceous though it might be, was not the issue. It was the size of her character, personality, heart and spirit that made him miss her with every part of his being.

So lost was he in his thoughts, the buzz of the intercom startled him. "Your Highness?"

He pushed the button to answer. "Yes?"

"Your wife has arrived."

Kardahl's heart lurched and a feeling of heightened anticipation surged through him. It took all of his considerable self-control to keep his voice level. "Send her in."

It seemed a lifetime before the office door opened and she stood there. In evening gown or jeans, she had never looked more beautiful to him than she did now wearing a floral print skirt, cream-colored blouse and loosely crocheted sweater. Her sunkissed brown hair was pulled into a casual knot at her nape with loose strands caressing her neck and cheeks. The blood pounded through his veins and roared in his ears as the need to take her in his arms became almost more than his considerable self-control could withstand.

He stood but did not come around to meet her. He kept his glass-topped desk between them. "Hello."

"Hi. This is nice," she said, looking around the spacious office with the thick Berber carpet and leather furniture. "I never saw where you work."

One corner of his mouth lifted. "You did not believe I worked so it would have been an exercise in futility."

"I was wrong." She pointed a finger at him. "And that's the last time I'm going to say it."

"Very well." He held out a hand, indicating the two chairs in front of his desk. "Please sit down."

"Thank you." Her tone was very formal now.

He preferred the seductive whisper in her voice when he had held her in his arms and made love to her. He favored the teasing tone just now when she had admitted her erroneous first impression of his character. He desired almost anything to the aloof and distancing manner she had assumed just a moment ago.

"I regret that my secretary did not put you through when you called earlier," he said. "I was involved. Had I but known you were trying to reach me, I would have interrupted the proceedings. It was a budget conference—" He stopped. Since when did he babble about trivialities? "To what do I owe the pleasure of your first visit to my office?"

"This is something I thought I should tell you in person."

The look on her face was difficult to read and he wondered when she had learned to mask her emotions so well. She had agreed to stay in Bha'Khar until she learned whether or not she carried his child. Since he had not seen or spoken to her in several weeks, it was an educated guess that her visit to the lion's den was in regard to her physical condition.

"Are you pregnant?" he asked bluntly.

She sighed. "No."

"No?"

She shook her head and he read the truth in her eyes. His spirits plummeted and until that moment he had not realized he had carried inside him a high level of anticipation that her answer would be different.

"I see," was all he said.

She looked surprised. "I thought you'd be more relieved."

As did he. But it was not so. He became conscious of the fact that he did indeed want a child with Jessica and the awareness stunned him.

Before he could formulate a response to that, she spoke again. "That's one hurdle out of the way."

"Of what?" he asked.

"Dissolution of our union. Since there can't be an annulment, we need to go ahead with the divorce."

As the words penetrated, again he was stunned. It was thickheaded of him to believe she would have changed her mind, but he realized the hope had been there all along.

"Have you spoken with your grandparents regarding your wishes?"

She nodded. "They're disappointed. They'd hoped I would stay in Bha'Khar, but ultimately they want me to be happy."

"Are you so very certain you cannot be happy here in the palace?"

"With you," she clarified.

"Yes." He did not wish to look deeply into his feelings, but one thing was quite clear. He did not want her to go. "I respect and care for you."

She clasped her hands in her lap and rubbed one thumb over the other. The gesture had become so familiar. She was nervous and he was glad.

"I've come to respect you, too, Kardahl. And that's saying a lot considering my opinion when I arrived."

"I am glad. Life here could be very rewarding. You could champion the causes of the desert people and there are children in Bha'Khar who would benefit greatly from your interest and support."

She shook her head. "It's not enough."

"Those two causes are quite a challenge," he argued. "You would—"

"That's not what I meant. It's not enough for me personally. I'm a hopeless romantic. Like my mother. All my life I've dreamed of being swept off my feet by the man of my dreams." She laughed self-consciously. "I know that sounds foolish, but it's the truth. And I won't settle for less."

Kardahl didn't know what to say. In the beginning, it had all seemed so simple. They would help each other. But that was before he had come to know her. And want her. And love…

No. Not that.

But he could not say the words that would keep her here. He was loath to think it let alone give weight

and importance by voicing it. That would tempt fate
and he just wished to go on as they were. His greatest
pain had been precipitated by this condition and he
would not let himself ever experience such a thing
again.

"I won't agree to a divorce," he ground out.

Her gaze jumped to his and something flashed in
her eyes. "Then you leave me no choice but to hire
an attorney, one whose specialty is international law."

"Is that a threat?"

"No. But the thing is, we both know I have a good
case for dissolving this marriage. I signed the proxy
under false pretenses."

"Have you been so unhappy in Bha'Khar?" he
demanded.

She hesitated for a split second. "That's not the
point," she finally said. "You've made it clear that
you can't love me. You'll never know how deeply I
wish it could be different. And how sorry I am for
you. And angry. To withhold your love is disrespect-
ful to the memory of the woman you lost and the
child who will never live except in your heart."

The truth of her words pierced his heart and he
winced at the pain. "Jessica, I—"

She stood. "The thing is, Kardahl, your heart is
dead. That means your child will never live at all.
And I won't be tied by a binding legal agreement to
a man who can't love me. That's no life at all."

CHAPTER TWELVE

KARDAHL stared at the divorce papers on his desk. It had only been a week since she had sat in the chair across from him and said that she would not be legally bound to a man who could not love her. He had made known his positive feelings. Why was that not enough for her? They got on so well together, why did she need more?

The intercom on his desk buzzed and he answered. "Yes?"

"The Crown Prince is here to see you, Your Highness."

"Send him in." Kardahl smiled. He knew what this was about and relished the opportunity to do battle with his brother.

Malik entered his office and sat down in front of the desk. He did not look happy. "Father sent me to speak with you. You are asking for a lot of money, Kardahl."

"Yes. But it will be well spent on programs that have been too long neglected."

His brother's gaze narrowed. "This is the first time you have expressed such a viewpoint."

With Jessica, it was the first time he had met such an extraordinary woman who had a way of cutting to the heart of a matter. He had been operating under the belief that he was handling his responsibilities as a member of the royal family. She had made him see that he was isolated and out of touch with the needs of the people. He was detached from life in general and simply going through the motions of his work without an emotional connection. That was not enough in order to be an effective public official whose primary interest should be the welfare of the citizens of Bha'Khar.

Kardahl linked his fingers and rested his hands on the divorce decree on his desk. "It has been brought to my attention that the government is not doing all it could and should to invest in the future of Bha'Khar."

A gleam stole into Malik's eyes. "Lately your attention has been concentrated on your wife. Would I be wrong to think that she is the one who has altered your views?"

"It does not matter. The point is that the allocation is necessary."

"I agree, but you are the minister of Finance. It is up to you to convince father to change his mind." Malik leaned his elbows on his knees and his look was sympathetic. "You know better than anyone that he holds in high esteem the traditions of the land of our birth."

"Sometimes traditions need shaking up." But with the power of passion for his cause, he would be persuasive. "I am prepared to change his mind."

"Are you prepared to forgive him also?"

Kardahl knew what his brother was asking. All this time he had held his father responsible for the tragedy that took the woman he had loved. The truth was, it was an accident and Kardahl had felt the need to hold someone accountable. Perhaps in time the king would have been convinced to alter the tradition and allow him to marry the mother of his child. They would never know. He would always have tender feelings for them, but the paralyzing pain no longer held him in a state somewhere between life and death. In truth, tradition had brought him Jessica. It was he, Kardahl, who had erred badly and he did not know how to make things right.

"Yes." He sighed. "I am no longer angry at father."

Malik nodded. "I suspect Jessica is responsible for this as well?"

"In a circuitous way."

"That heartens me," his brother said, smiling broadly. "My own betrothed will be here from America in a number of weeks."

"Tread cautiously with your optimism. You know the circumstances of our marriage?"

"That father's overzealous aide obtained her signature on the proxy in a deceptive manner? Yes. I heard."

Kardahl held up the legal document. "And you know that she is determined to obtain a divorce."

"I do. And you do not wish it?"

"No."

"That is a problem. You seem confident of persuading father of the wisdom of your budget allocations. Yet you cannot convince your wife of the wisdom of remaining married to you?" The gleam in Malik's eyes was clear evidence that he was enjoying this far too much.

"The two matters are completely unrelated." As, at the moment, he wished he and his brother were.

"I will be certain not to make the same mistakes when my own bride arrives. Although, I am assured that the bride chosen for me is well-trained in the matters of discipline, royal protocol and tradition. And, unlike your wife, she is obedient."

"You are in for a rude awakening, my brother," Kardahl assured him. "Obedience does not guarantee a successful marriage."

"It does not hurt."

Hurt. Kardahl sighed. Both he and Jessica were wounded souls. She was a young and vulnerable witness to her mother's downward fall into alcoholism while searching for love. He had found it once, only to have it ripped away, making him determined not to care or hurt again. What a pair they were.

He refused to debate the virtues of an obedient bride. Soon enough his brother would deal with the issue on his own. But Kardahl did wish to unburden himself as the knot of pain inside him would not go away. Maybe Jessica was right and talking would help.

"Jessica has longed for a romantic relationship and will not settle for less than her expectation." He met his brother's gaze. "And I have stubbornly resisted loving again."

"To no avail," his brother commented.

As much as he disliked feeding his brother's ego, he could not deny the truth of the statement. "You would be correct."

"Then you must talk her out of the divorce," Malik said seriously.

"How do you suggest I do that?"

"Convince her of your deep and tender feelings."

"I have shown her in every possible way that I care. So, again I say, how do I go about that?" Kardahl demanded.

"You have a certain reputation with the ladies—"

"Do not go there." This was not the time to inform his brother that reminding Jessica of his reputation would be counterproductive to his goal of changing her mind.

"Let me finish. I'm simply suggesting that you should do what you do best. Court her. As I intend to do with my betrothed when she arrives."

"Flowers? Moonlight? Promises?" Cold showers in a mountain stream, he thought with a shudder. Lying beside her without touching when all he wanted was to pull her into his arms and kiss her until neither of them could think straight.

"Exactly," his brother agreed.

"She is not susceptible to traditional courting methods."

"If they were accompanied by a sincere declaration of your feelings that might alter her perception," Malik pointed out. He leaned back in the chair and steepled his fingers as he studied Kardahl. "If you love her and I feel certain that is the case, you must tell her so."

"I cannot."

"Rubbish."

Kardahl stood and started pacing his office. "It would test the boundaries of fate. The last time I said those words to a woman I lost her."

"It seems to me that you will lose again if you do not say it." Malik stood and stepped into his path, making him stop, meeting his gaze to get his point across. "This time the loss would be unforgivable because it is within your power to control."

Kardahl felt the air leave his lungs as surely as if his brother had made a fist and punched him in the stomach. All this time he had been trying to control his feelings because that was the only thing he had power over. Except with Jessica, he had no power to resist her. She forced him to feel again and he was in love with her.

He hoped he had not realized the truth of his feelings too late.

* * *

Excitement raced through Jessica as she walked into the palace ballroom filled with men and women wearing tuxedos and gowns. She'd dressed with great care in a floor-length strapless black satin dress and her grandparents thought she looked beautiful. They were here somewhere, hanging out with their friends the king and queen of Bha'Khar, soon to be her ex-in-laws. The ball was held annually to celebrate national pride and when Kardahl had called and invited her to one last palace function, she hadn't been able to refuse him. His charm had nothing to do with her decision to attend. Being in love with him had everything to do with it.

Foolishly she'd once thought that if he told her he cared it would be enough. The last time she'd seen him he'd said the words, but it wasn't all right. She didn't want just all right, she wanted fireworks and moonbeams.

She stood just inside the door as the royal family took their places on a dais at the front of the ballroom. The king made a speech and said the world was changing and Bha'khar needed energy and youth to guide it into the world order. He planned to step aside soon to let Prince Malik assume the throne with the counsel of his brother Prince Kardahl.

Even the sound of his name made Jessica's heart beat faster. She was going to miss him terribly. And not only him. She would miss the country, the people, her family. The downside of knowing them was having to say goodbye. As she watched, Kardahl stepped to the microphone. He was a sight for sore eyes and an even sorer heart. As if he had a special radar, his gaze met hers across the crowded room and he smiled the smile that made her stomach drop and her knees weak.

"Good evening. My parents, my brother and I thank you all for coming tonight." He glanced at his father and the two exchanged a smile. Then Kardahl looked into the crowd, finally meeting her gaze. "Someone whose opinion I respect very much recently pointed out to me that I have been neglecting our most precious natural resource. That ends tonight. The king has approved my proposal to appropriate a great deal of money for educational endeavors for the children of Bha'Khar. I will personally oversee the dispersal of these funds. But talk is cheap. It is action that shows the sincerity of a man's heart. If I do not fulfill this promise, I expect the citizens of the country to hold me accountable as I shall hold myself accountable." After a burst of sudden and enthusiastic applause tapered off, he said, "We are here tonight to celebrate. Our country has long and distinguished traditions. Talking is one of them, but I have done enough for tonight. On behalf of the king and queen and the Crown Prince I wish you all to enjoy yourselves."

Stunned didn't begin to describe what Jessica was feeling. Kardahl had been talking about her. He respected her. He'd told her so, when he'd said he cared. Tonight he'd said so publicly. And he was right. Actions spoke louder than words. Everything he'd done said he cared and she'd thrown that away.

She looked up and saw that he was coming toward her, making his way through the crowd. Her first thought was to run and that was exactly why she stood her ground and smiled when he finally stood in front of her.

"Hello," she said.

"You came."

"I did. And I see that you've been busy making up with your father and finding money for the kids."

He grinned. "The king and I have indeed come to a new and pleasant understanding. After much discussion he saw the wisdom of investing in the youth of Bha'Khar."

"I'm so glad, Kardahl," she said.

His smile disappeared and a fierce intensity darkened his eyes. "I must speak with you alone."

"All right." How could she say no? She wanted nothing more than to be alone with him—even if it was for the last time. Especially because of that.

He took her arm and they slipped out the door and into the hall. Just outside, a group of reporters waited, like circling sharks who smelled blood in the water and were waiting to pounce. He put his arm around her and they continued to walk as questions peppered them.

"There's a rumor that your marriage is falling apart. Would you care to comment?"

"Your Highness, we heard your speech. Did your wife talk you into appropriating the money for the kids?"

"She's a social worker in the United States, right? Can you confirm that she grew up in a state run home?

"Is it also true that her mother died of alcoholism?"

Kardahl turned on them, his lean jaw tight with fury. "My wife has the greatest heart of any woman I have ever known. I will confirm what is public record and that is that she has known some adversity. Without that, she would not be as beautiful on the inside as she is on the outside."

A microphone was thrust at him. "Would you care to comment on the state of your marriage?"

When he answered, his voice was hard as steel. "My wife made me think about many things. And she is responsible for the fact that I have put aside my selfish ways. She made me want to be a better man. But hear me, and hear me well—I need you, all of the media to spread my message for the children. But I will tolerate no further intrusion into my private life. Do I make myself clear?"

Jess was as speechless as the reporters. Before any of them could answer, he took her hand in a firm grasp and escorted her down the hall and to the elevators. He pushed the button for the ground floor. The next thing she knew, they were in the palace garden. This was where Kardahl had kissed her for the first time. The lighting and lush plants had made it magical then, and the memories made it even more magical now. Sadness swamped her at the thought of leaving everything she'd ever wanted. She'd been too angry and defensive to recognize it, to fight for it.

He held out his arm, indicating the wrought-iron bench. "Will you sit with me?"

"Yes."

One word was all she could manage since her throat was thick with emotion. So much for going away quietly. The press had dug into her past and it would be out there for all the world to see. But once again, Kardahl had been there for her, defending her. And the things he'd said... More importantly, the things he was going to do. Suddenly the feelings grew so big she couldn't hold them back. A single tear slipped from the corner of her eye. Then another. And another.

"Jessica—" He cupped her cheek in his hand and brushed the moisture away with his thumb. "The reporters will not bother you again. I will not allow it."

She shook her head. "That's not why I'm crying."

"Tell me who is responsible for your unhappiness and I will see that they are severely punished."

"You are responsible."

"I?" If she'd slapped him, he couldn't have looked more surprised.

She nodded. "You're going to use your power for good. For the children."

"I was under the impression that is what you wished."

"I do. And it makes me very happy."

Confusion creased his forehead. "I do not understand. If you are happy, then why do you cry?"

"I'm sad, too. You would have been an amazing father."

She had nothing left to lose by telling him that. Since the day she'd told him she wasn't carrying his child, she'd had a lot of time to think about things. How her mother must have felt—pregnant, alone, scared. And in love with a man she could never have. But knowing love once made her want the feeling again and she had looked, but was doomed to the disappointment of never finding it. Loving Kardahl, wanting to be with him and only him, made Jessica understand. The power of love, the unbelievably wonderful feeling was why her mother had kept searching to find it again.

Something inside Jess melted away and she suspected it was bitterness she hadn't even known she carried. She hadn't realized she needed to forgive her mother, but she felt the burden of resentment lift from her heart.

Kardahl took her hand in both of his. "I am pleased that you think I would be a good father. But I find myself in need of a woman who would be a good mother."

Her gaze jumped to his as hope swelled inside

her. What if just once life came down on the side of the hopeless romantic? But what if she was wrong?

"It's too late, Kardahl. The divorce is proceeding. Maybe it would be better just to let it go on. Maybe we'd be better off apart—"

"No." His eyes were fierce and stubborn determination pressed his mouth into a thin line. "I cannot speak for you, but I know for certain that I would *not* be better off."

"But we—"

"I love you," he said simply.

"What?" She couldn't believe her ears weren't substituting words that her heart desperately wanted to hear.

"You can go through with severing our union, but that will not end it. I will continue to pursue you and as you have pointed out on numerous occasions, I have had much practice in successfully pursuing women."

"There is a saying—never judge a book by its cover. I am guilty of that. I didn't know you or understand what you'd been through. I didn't realize that you were capable of deep and lasting feelings. And now—"

"Now, my darling, I am in love with you. I have courted and won many who were unimportant, but I love only you. That makes you beyond important, it makes you priceless."

She struggled against all her perceptions honed by sadness and loss. "It's difficult for me to believe—"

He touched a finger to her lips to silence her.

"Believe it. You are the one who breathed life into my soul once again. You are the one who brought me out of the shadows. Your fingers touched my unresponsive heart and pulled it free of the dark place where I have hidden it to keep it safe. And now that I have begun to feel again, I can no longer be satisfied with this empty life I have known."

"Oh, Kardahl—"

He took her face in his hands and there was a desperation in his touch, in his gaze. "If you do not return my feelings now, at least give me another chance. I will do everything within my power to change your mind—"

"I do love you."

He went completely still, then slowly a smile relaxed the tension in his mouth. "That pleases me." Lowering his head, he touched his lips to hers in the most exquisite kiss. When he pulled away, he said, "I am humbled and honored. And very grateful."

Then he went down on one knee as he slid his hand into his pocket and pulled out a ring. "Your courage and spirit in facing life are an inspiration and I wish to be your equal, to embrace life with you by my side. This ring has been in my family for generations and it is fitting that one who knows the fragility and value of family be the one to wear it." He met her gaze with an earnest sincerity that took her breath away. "Will you do me the honor of being my wife?"

"It's the most beautiful ring I've ever seen." She

was dazzled by the sapphire surrounded by diamonds as he slipped it on her finger. Then she smiled into his eyes. "I'm already your wife."

"I wish to have a ceremony, an exchange of vows—face-to-face this time. Vows spoken with the love we have found through the tradition of betrothal by our beloved families, the love we will share for the rest of our lives. Will you do that?"

"I will."

He stood and pulled her to her feet and into his arms. "Oh, my heart, you have made me the happiest man in the world."

She rested her cheek on his chest and heard the solid steady beat of the heart she'd brought back to life. A happiness she'd never known before expanded inside her. "You're a good man, so different from what I thought at first. Now I know you simply lost your way for a while."

"And you have shown me the path to contentment."

"Right back at you. Nothing would make me happier than to be your wife and have children with you. Together we can make the world a better place."

He nodded. "It is my solemn promise to my reluctant bride."

She wasn't reluctant any longer. She was a hopeless romantic who'd found the love of her life halfway around the world and validated what she'd always believed.

Love will find a way.

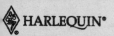
HARLEQUIN®

American ROMANCE®

A THREE-BOOK SERIES BY BELOVED AUTHOR

Judy Christenberry

Dallas Duets
What's behind the doors of
the Yellow Rose Lane apartments?
Love, Texas-style!

THE MARRYING KIND
May 2007

Jonathan Davis was many things—a millionaire,
a player, a catch. But he'd never be a husband.
For him, "marriage" equaled "mistake." Diane Black
was a forever kind of woman, a babies-and-minivan
kind of woman. But John was confident he could
date her and still avoid that trap.
Until he kissed her…

Also watch for:

DADDY NEXT DOOR
January 2007

MOMMY FOR A MINUTE
August 2007

Available wherever Harlequin books are sold.

www.eHarlequin.com
HARM07JC

REQUEST YOUR FREE BOOKS!
2 FREE NOVELS PLUS 2
FREE GIFTS!

HARLEQUIN ROMANCE®

From the Heart, For the Heart

HR07

Coming Next Month

#3949 THE SHERIFF'S PREGNANT WIFE Patricia Thayer
Rocky Mountain Brides
Surprise is an understatement for Sheriff Reed Larkin when he finds out
his childhood sweetheart has returned home. After all these years
Paige Keenan's smile can still make his heart ache. But what's the secret
he can see in her whiskey-colored eyes?

#3950 THE PRINCE'S OUTBACK BRIDE Marion Lennox
Prince Max de Gautier travels to the Australian Outback in search of the heir
to the throne. But Max finds a feisty woman who is fiercely protective of her
adopted children. Although Pippa is wary of this dashing prince, she agrees
to spend one month in his royal kingdom.

#3951 THE SECRET LIFE OF LADY GABRIELLA Liz Fielding
Lady Gabriella March is the perfect domestic goddess—but in truth
she's simply Ellie March, who uses the beautiful mansion she is house-
sitting to inspire her writing. The owner returns, and Ellie discovers that
Dr. Benedict Faulkner is the opposite of the aging academic she'd imagined.

#3952 BACK TO MR & MRS Shirley Jump
Makeover Bride & Groom
Cade and Melanie were the high school prom king and queen. Twenty years
on, Cade realizes that he let work take over and has lost the one person
who lit up his world. Now he is determined to show Melanie he can be the
husband she needs...and win back her heart.

#3953 MEMO: MARRY ME? Jennie Adams
Since her accident, and her problems with remembering things, working in
an office can sometimes be hard for Lily Kellaway. But with the new boss,
Zach Swift, it feels different. And not just because he is seriously gorgeous!
Now he has asked her to join him on a business trip.

#3954 HIRED BY THE COWBOY Donna Alward
Western Weddings
Alexis Grayson has always looked after herself. So what if she is alone and
pregnant? Gorgeous cowboy Connor Madsen seems determined to take
care of her. And he needs something from her, too—a temporary wife! But
soon Alexis realizes she wants to be a *real* wife to Connor.

HRCNM0407